A DANGEROUS DESCENT

A Sarah McKinney Mystery

Copyright © 2015 Marian Exall. All rights reserved.

ISBN: 9781511723602

This is a work of fiction. Any resemblance to actual persons, living or dead, or to actual events or locales is entirely coincidental

ACKNOWLEDGMENTS

Many people helped me with this novel. Seth Zimmerman fact-checked the New York chapters, and Sally Dollé corrected my French language usage and reviewed my references to French police and criminal procedure. Any remaining errors are my fault. Oona Sherman Cava, Jolene Hansen, Pam Helberg, Dawn Landau and Lynn McKinster, wicked women writers all, generously contributed their time, skills and life experiences, as I alternately skipped and slogged, chapter by chapter, towards the final paragraph. I couldn't have done it without them. Thanks also go to Sandy Oitzinger for her encouraging early read, and especially to Rob and Rachel Gray whose hospitality at their *maison secondaire* introduced me to the Dordogne region, and inspired the setting of this novel. Finally, I am grateful to my husband Graham, my first and most appreciative reader.

A DANGEROUS DESCENT

A Sarah McKinney Mystery

CHAPTER 1

New York - Monday

I didn't love New York. At least, I didn't love it at five-thirty p.m. on the hottest early June day on record. I lingered in the air-conditioned hush of the law firm lobby, reluctant to fight my way onto the subway from Wall Street to my hotel in midtown. There I would change, then join the rush hour struggle again back downtown to Little Italy for my unfashionably early dinner date. Instead, I made up my mind to walk the dozen blocks north. The exercise would do me good, and burn off some of the frustration accumulated throughout a day of mediation going nowhere fast. I peeled off my suit jacket and started to weave my way through the crowds on lower Broadway, keeping to the shade of the buildings. I cut across to Foley Square, maintaining a decent pace, but earning a couple of dirty looks and a "watch it, lady!" from other pedestrians. The traffic was jammed solid on Canal Street, tempers rising with the temperature, as commuters headed for home in Brooklyn and points east. I made it to Mulberry Street by six p.m., a little sweaty but mentally cleansed.

The restaurant – Giovanni's – had little to distinguish it from the others in the area: a similar window display of demijohns of olive oil, set amongst an arrangement of vine leaves and wax grapes, whole hams hanging in a screen above. But if Sam Cantor had selected it, I bet it was one of the best. Sam had lived in New York all his sixty-plus years, and he shared my love of good food and wine. I entered the restaurant and stood relishing the cool and quiet, unfazed by the lack of anyone to greet me. Ahead was a corridor that probably led to the dining room. To my right, a small dark space that I guessed housed the bar. No one in it. Distant sounds reached me, silverware chinking against china, a raised voice from the kitchen. I breathed in a mixture of comforting cooking smells.

A short bald man in a tuxedo bustled up the corridor towards me.

"I'm so sorry you had to wait! Is it dinner for one?"

"Actually, I'm meeting someone. I'm just early. He probably made a reservation? Sam Cantor?"

"Ah, *Signore* Cantor! Of course, he's an old friend. Please, take a seat in the bar while you wait. We're just opening up."

He escorted me into the room on the right, turned on a couple of table lamps, then hurried behind the bar, where he engaged in an elaborate display of bottle and glass juggling. He emerged again with a champagne flute filled with a cloudy yellow liquid, decorated with a sprig of mint.

"Our signature cocktail, the Giovanni, with the compliments of the house."

"What's in it?"

"Just limoncello and prosecco. It's absolutely harmless; perfect for a hot day like today."

I didn't believe it was harmless for a minute, but it did look delicious. My host took his leave, and I relaxed into the sofa cushions, sipping my drink, thinking about Sam and his late wife Marta.

A decade earlier, I had been employed as an associate at a prestigious New York law firm. I had signed up for a course at NYU Law School on alternative dispute resolution taught by Marta Cantor. The subject matter of the course interested me less than that it took place on Saturday, nominally not a work day, and would fulfill a significant portion of my annual Continuing Legal Education requirement. Like my peers, I worked sixty-hour weeks, and thought I'd be lucky to attend two out of the three sessions. I was hooked after the first class, especially when Marta introduced us to mediation, and I moved heaven and earth to keep my next two Saturdays free. After three years toiling in the trenches of the litigation department, I already knew there had to be a better way to resolve disputes than the time-consuming, expensive and arbitrary "courtroom" method. Not that any of the cases I worked on came close to trial. They were fought as a war of attrition through endless discovery, interspersed by the filing of lengthy motions which served no purpose other than to drive up legal fees until one party or the other cried "uncle."

A dynamic teacher, more a professor of psychology than law, Marta showed us how to strip away the disputants' contesting legal positions in order to reveal their underlying fundamental interests, then to help them brainstorm a solution which satisfied all parties. It was heady stuff after a week of pouring over thousands of pages of documents in the hope of finding a misplaced comma. When, at the end of the course, she offered the opportunity to volunteer at the Queens Dispute Resolution Center, a non-profit headed by her husband, I signed up.

Marta and Sam were complete opposites. She was short, plump and feisty. Her classroom presentations were laced with drama and humor, as she took on the voices of the parties to the conflict she was describing. Her raven hair – dyed, I was sure – was cut in a severe bob, and she applied scarlet lipstick inexpertly to her wide mouth. Smears of it could be seen on her teeth as she launched into her lecture. She dressed exclusively in red and black, giving the impression of an eccentric priest as she strode and spun in front of her bewitched students.

Sam looked far more the professor than his wife. He personified the absent-minded academic with his halo of white Albert Einstein curls around a domed forehead that stretched back forever and gleamed with the assurance of the grey matter it enclosed. He stood tall and stooped, prone to soft tweeds and sweaters in earthy shades that hung off him, as if he had bought them at some jumble sale without much regard to size.

Marta inspired me, but over the ensuing months, soft-spoken Sam nurtured the idea that I might actually build a practice exclusively doing mediation. With Sam as my guide and mentor, I learned how to listen, how to ask those questions that burrowed behind the zero-sum, "I win, you lose" game. After the dry corporate world of securities fraud and intellectual property disputes, it seemed more authentic and meaningful. First as an observer, then as co-mediator with Sam, and finally, as sole mediator under his supervision, I witnessed the magic of the process.

Sam encouraged me to trust that process, and to trust myself. After I left New York to move back to Atlanta where I had gone to law school, we kept in touch. In the early days, he advised me and referred other attorneys to me who might be amenable to mediation. When I visited New York, I always made a point of having dinner with him and Marta either at their NYU-owned apartment or one of the fantastic ethnic restaurants in the neighborhood. This would be the first time I had seen him since her funeral the previous December.

Gradually, the restaurant came to life. Customers moved through to the dining room. A couple joined me in the bar, where a white-coated barman materialized to see to their needs. My glass had emptied and been miraculously replaced with a full one when the door to the street opened again, and Sam came through, peering to left and right while adjusting to the dimness of the interior. His slow entrance gave me a chance to assess him before he saw me, and to hide my shock at his appearance. Always slim, he now was gaunt, and the absent-minded professor had given way to a more disheveled look: he wouldn't have been out of place begging for change in Washington Square. He had looked stricken at the funeral; now he looked haunted.

He spotted me and smiled. I hurried across the bar and hugged him hard, hiding my face in his chest to mask the tears that filled my eyes. To me, this man was much closer to a dad than my biological father. I hated to see him so hollowed out with grief, but my tears would do him no good at this moment. As soon as I could manage, I smiled up at him.

"It's so good to see you."

"You too. You look wonderful."

The arrival of the maître d' protected me from giving the stock response, which would have been patently untrue.

"Giovanni, thanks for looking after Sarah." Turning back to me, "I hope you haven't been waiting long."

As we followed Giovanni back to the dining room and were seated, I explained about the mediation and my decision to walk up to Little Italy, rather than return to my hotel and change.

"I didn't mind the wait. It gave me a chance to relax and process the day."

That led to a discussion about my current case. As always, Sam's perceptions were astute, and his face came to life a little as we explored several avenues to probe the next day that might break the deadlock gripping the parties. On the face of it, the case concerned a will dispute with millions of dollars at stake, but as always, the underlying conflict had less to do with money than unmet needs: the second wife's need for recognition and respect from the deceased's adult children; the son's need to free himself of the corporate straitjacket he had donned to please his father; the daughter's simple need for affection. The family was a mess, not in the obvious way my family had been a mess -- with drugs, violence and poverty – but with the silent screaming tension of the dysfunctional rich. I wasn't going to fix it, but perhaps, as Sam had taught me, I could help these survivors start to recognize where their long-term interests lay.

By the time we had demolished a shared platter of *antipasto misto* – home-cured charcuterie, fresh mozzarella, bruschetta with eggplant and tomato – the talk had moved on to the Queens Dispute Resolution Center, as always struggling for funding.

"So when are you going to start a dispute resolution center down in Atlanta?" Sam asked. He had encouraged me to get involved in the non-profit area of conflict resolution several times before.

"Oh, Sam, I'm not sure Georgia's ready for the touchy-feely stuff you do. It all sounds like psychobabble to Southerners. I *am* teaching a course on alternative dispute resolution at the law school next semester, and that might lead to a clinic with student interns, and that might lead .... somewhere."

We lapsed into silence. Our main courses arrived. The dining room was noisy now, voices rising and falling, sudden bursts of laughter, the good cheer of people enjoying superb food and wine. I watched the animation drain from Sam's face as he fingered the stem of his glass. As I searched for another topic to enliven him again, Giovanni stopped by our table with a refill of the excellent Barolo he had recommended. Sam beat me to the punch.

"Are you still seeing that journalist guy?"

My fork stopped half-way between the seafood risotto and my mouth.

"Why?"

"Isn't he based in Paris?"

We smiled sheepishly at each other, recognizing that we had both employed the familiar evasive technique of answering a question with a question. I made a pretense of chewing a mouthful that in fact had melted on impact, while I pondered my response to his original question.

I hadn't "seen" Pieter Dykstra since we parted at Atlanta's Hartsfield-Jackson Airport the previous October. There had been one uncomfortable three-way telephone call with his book editor on the line, during which we had hammered out an agreement to delete my name and all identifying references to me in "*The Riddle of the Sphinx*," the book that had been rushed into print about Dykstra's search for the hidden assets of Middle-Eastern strongmen. We had met in the course of his investigation, and I had become involved in the bloody later stages. Our affair had been short and intense, fueled – I was now convinced – as much by the surrounding danger as mutual attraction. Still, I couldn't count the number of times I had taken out the review copy the publisher sent me. I had flicked through the pages, lighting on one page then another, trying to hear his voice in the crisp journalistic prose used to lay out the story, then turning to the back cover to stare at his photograph.

"He's based in London actually. We're not in contact, but I could put you in touch with him. Why?" I repeated.

This time it was Sam who paused.

"I thought he might help me find my daughter."

My mouth dropped open. "But you don't— ! You and Marta never had children!"

"No, she's not Marta's. I was married before."

I stared at him, waiting for more. He started hesitantly, his delivery staccato, until he eased into his narrative.

"1968, I was about to graduate from Columbia. Parents wanted me to go on to law school. Prolong the draft deferment. I wasn't keen. SDS – that's Students for a Democratic Society – sent me to Paris." He leant across the table, holding my wrist for a moment. "Sarah, you can't imagine what it was like back then. Campuses everywhere were alight with protest. Not just the Vietnam War, the whole damn order was in question. And nowhere more than Paris. Workers and students unite! It was really happening! We were within a blink of revolution!"

He leaned back again, his eyes now drifting unfocused across the room. He was back there in Paris, in 1968. I tried to imagine what he looked like then: dark and intense, lit with the fire of conviction.

"I lived with a group from the Sorbonne. During the day we went to the factories in the suburbs to speak with union members. At night, we talked and argued, smoked and drank red wine, made love ….. I had an affair with a woman called Claire; she looked like Joan Baez, even played the guitar." He gave a wry chuckle.

"Then it all came apart. The students and the workers split. The police cracked down. My parents wrote and told me I'd been accepted at NYU Law School, and I came home. Half-way through my first semester, Claire wrote to say she was pregnant. She had lost some of her revolutionary zeal too; returned to the bourgeoisie she came from, I guess. She wanted to marry. My parents said they'd help us. I don't know what her parents thought; I never spoke to them. So, she came to New York, and we got married. Chantal was born in March 1969.

"It was pretty bad. I was working full-time to keep a roof over our heads, as well as struggling to keep up with classes. Claire hated New York, couldn't learn English, and didn't get on with my folks. Anyway, after a year, she took the baby back to her parents' home in Limoges. I sent money; Claire sent photos, at least to start with."

"Did Marta know?" I asked. I knew they had met in the final year of law school and married after graduation.

"Oh, yes. We had no secrets. Marta encouraged me to write to Chantal. She picked out presents for me to send on Chantal's birthdays. She arranged for us to go to France to visit. Chantal was eleven then. That was the last time I saw her: a strange, quiet child, always clinging to her mother. I think Claire poisoned the well for me. After that visit, the letters went unanswered, the presents and money unacknowledged. Eventually, I … just gave up. The only word I've had from Chantal since is this."

He pulled a much-fingered envelope from his inside jacket pocket and handed it to me. Inside was a death announcement, in French, for Claire Dubenoit. The date of death was November 4, 2010, the previous November, when I had been licking my wounds in Atlanta, and Sam had been caring round the clock for his cancer-ridden wife. I handed it back. Sam stowed it, and took a swallow of wine. He braced

his shoulders for w
of the story. He kep.

"When Mar\
find Chantal, to recor.
and they were brimm.
commandment. I—"

He broke off, o\
the table, and waited until

"I went to France,
address on the card." He ge
placed the announcement. "
had moved to the country. To
in Dordogne. I went there, bu.   .ne old
woman next door – it's an old s   . aivided in two
– seemed to know something.   ..ixed about "Madame"
and pointed to the other half of the building, but I couldn't
understand her accent. She gave me a key, and I went inside.
I couldn't find anything to tell me where Chantal had gone.
The place didn't even look lived in, too clean and tidy."
Sam's words ran together now, the remembered frustration he
had experienced at the farmhouse speeding up his delivery. "I
forgot to return the key, so I went back the next day. The old
woman wasn't home, and I thought I'd have a last look
around Chantal's place to see if I had missed something. I
was standing in the main room when a man came down the
stairs and walked straight past me. I called after him, but he
just disappeared around the end of the buildings. I supposed
he had a car parked down the lane somewhere."

"Who was he?"

"No idea. Long dark hair in a ponytail, that's all I
saw."

"What did you do then?"

"I went to the police in St. Barthélemy, that's the
nearest town, but they weren't very interested. Said they
couldn't treat Chantal as a missing person with the facts I'd
given them. They said they'd send someone to talk to the old
lady, but I doubt they did. I left my contact information, but
I've heard nothing. I had to come back to work."

...a can help?"

...might have sources that could ...touch with a private investigator in ...could track Chantal down?"

...e a story in this for Dykstra, but thought he ...a phone call with Sam to advise him on next

"I'll give him your phone number, and ask him to call ...u." I had to admit to a small thrill of pleasure at having this excuse to reach out to him.

Sam seemed spent by the effort of recounting his history. My mind teemed with questions: about Sam, the revolutionary at the barricades of student revolt in Paris; and Sam and Marta, struggling to sustain a relationship with a little stranger five thousand miles away. This was not the moment to ask them. The parallels with my own history reverberated in my mind as we waited for the check: Chantal would be only a little older than me; both of us had rejected our American father, and grew up in Europe (me in England, her in France); and it sounded as if she was also single and childless.

It was still light when we emerged from the restaurant, although the heat had moderated some. The streets were crowded. New York accents fought with car horns and a street musician warbling a schmaltzy "*O Sole Mio*," hand pressed to heart. We walked to the corner to maximize my chance for a cab. Sam's apartment was only a few blocks away near NYU. I hated to think of him returning there alone with his grief and the added burden of this *mitzvah* to find his daughter. I turned and hugged him fiercely, for the second time that evening hiding my sudden tears against his chest.

"We'll find her, I promise," I whispered into his shirtfront.

***

Half an hour later, I was shivering in my fifteenth floor Midtown hotel room. The maid had cranked up the air-conditioning in my absence. While I waited for the temperature to normalize, I sat with my back against the headboard of the king-sized bed, legs stretched out in front, staring at Dykstra's contact information on my phone's screen. It was after two in the morning in London. I could picture Dykstra's flat, although I had only been there once; the stunning view over the Thames to St. Paul's and the City was hard to forget. His phone would probably be turned off. I could just leave a message, briefly reciting the facts and giving Sam's number. I felt a mixture of relief and disappointment at the realization I might not talk to him. Our relationship was complicated. After my chaotic childhood, I liked to be in control of my life. With Dykstra, I lost that control.

I punched in the numbers, rehearsing my message in my head. He answered on the first ring.

"Hello?"

I gulped, trying to disguise it as a cough.

"Hi, I'm so sorry. Did I wake you? It's Sarah. I thought I'd leave a message."

"Sarah!" He pronounced it the French way, with a long 'ah' sound on the first A, like a sigh. "It's early. I'm not asleep."

"Where are you? Not in London?"

"No, I'm here in America, the same time zone as Atlanta. It's so good to hear your voice."

"I'm in New York right now, but—"

"That's great! So am I. What hotel are you staying at?"

"The Marriott on Fifth and—"

"I know it. I'll see you in the Lobby Bar in fifteen minutes. I'm staying at the Domino. It's very close." He had named one of New York's trendiest boutique hotels. The journalism business must be good.

"But I just wanted to put you in touch with a friend of mine. There's no need to come over."

"Tell me all about it when I see you. Can't wait."

17

He had disconnected before I had a chance to protest further. Fifteen minutes: time to brush my hair and redo my make-up. Should I change? Stop it! This is not a date, I told myself. Perhaps just a dab of perfume ….?

Chapter 2

New York – Monday

The Marriott's Lobby Bar is vast and always crowded, yet Dykstra had managed to snag a table by the plate glass windows that looked down onto Fifth Avenue. He also managed to attract a waitress over.

"Just a coffee for me. Black." I'd had enough wine at dinner, and some nagging voice at the back of my head told me I should keep my wits about me.

"Maker's Mark, please. No ice." He wore a pale grey, short-sleeved shirt in a silky fabric, and black pants; casual but obviously European. I was glad I had, after all, changed from my charcoal pin-stripe business suit to a cream linen shift that showed off my toned biceps – I had recently supplemented my running with weights in an effort to fight the underarm sag that is the first sign of age.

He complimented me on my shorter haircut. I said I liked his new longer look. He smiled. The grin was unchanged and it had the same effect on me as it had the preceding Fall. I tried to suppress my response by concentrating on the traffic streaming by below the window. I had nearly lost my life because of that smile. My world was now back in equilibrium. I needed to hold onto my hard-won emotional independence, and keep this meeting merely friendly.

I brought my eyes back to his. "So, what brings you to New York? Are you following a story for Europ News?" That was the press agency he worked for.

"I'm doing a book tour for *The Riddle of the Sphinx*: ten cities in eleven days. It's going to be hell. Morning radio, then local TV interview, reading and signing in the evening. Would you like to come with me?"

I laughed off his invitation nervously.

"When do you start?"

"Here. Tomorrow."

"Would you have time sometime during the day to talk to a friend of mine? He's looking for some help with a missing person search in France."

I recited the pertinent facts. I left out the student revolutionary part, as well as Marta and the *mitzvah*. I described Sam as an old friend who had helped me get started in the mediation business.

He paused to think.

"Hmm. Sure, I'll be happy to speak to him. I have a few hours free tomorrow afternoon before the first read-and-sign. I can do a little internet research before I call him."

I gave him Sam's name and number, and we moved on to other topics: the situation in the Middle East, his recent travels, my recent cases, even the current heat wave. I had forgotten how easy it was to talk to him. He had an enormous range of knowledge but he never dropped names or sought to impress with inside information. He gave me his full attention, asked astute questions but avoided seeming to interrogate. I finally relaxed and enjoyed his company. While we batted subjects to and fro, I imagined his life in the months since we had been together. I could picture him hanging out with his international journalist colleagues, world-weary travelers in cargo pants and safari jackets; men -- and women too -- who could pack a duffel and board a plane for the other side of the world on a minute's notice. Such a contrast to my life, anchored firmly in place, with business trips minutely planned and scheduled weeks in advance. Another reason to steer clear of him, or a model for a richer, more fulfilling existence? I also couldn't help wondering if he was seeing someone. After all, I had no claim on him. I pictured one of those weather-beaten but beautiful women I glimpsed on CNN, reporting from Benghazi or Kabul, and tried to feel glad for him.

When I glanced at my watch, I was surprised to see it was nearly eleven.

"Well, I have a full day of mediation tomorrow, and now I really must get to bed." I immediately felt a schoolgirl blush moving up my neck, and I cursed my fair Scots-Irish complexion for the umpteenth time. Suddenly, the dangerous sexual electricity was back.

I was keenly aware of his body just a few inches from mine as he trailed me towards the elevator banks. We stood watching the floor numbers light up above the doors. Another couple stood silently beside us. A soft bell announced the arrival of an elevator. I stepped to the side to allow the others to enter, then turned to give Dykstra a quick farewell hug. I felt his lips brush my cheek.

He whispered, "Sarah, can I come up?"

I panicked. My self-composure crumbled.

"No!" I squeaked and rushed into the elevator. I kept my eyes tight shut until I heard the click of the doors coming together and felt the whoosh as I started my rise to the fifteenth floor. When I opened them, I saw my fellow travelers exchange meaningful smirks. They exited on the eighth floor, leaving me mentally kicking myself. After all, hadn't the possibility of sleeping with Dykstra been at the back of my mind ever since I told Sam in the restaurant that I'd contact him? I was only fooling myself when I pretended I would just voice-mail him and leave it at that. If I truly didn't want to get involved with him again, I never would have gone down to the bar.

I pulled my phone out of my purse as I left the elevator, searching for the most recent number called. Again, he answered on the first ring.

"It's Room 1545."

***

Dykstra left before five to go back to shower and change at his hotel before a local news radio interview. I didn't go back to sleep. I stood at the window, watching the grey light become gold. The sun reflected off the fancy peak of the Chrysler Building, and in the distance, if I craned my head way to the left, I could see slivers of the East River turning to silver between the buildings.

I tried to sort out my feelings about what had happened: the age-old war between heart and head. I didn't trust my heart. It had never had much exercise. From an early age I had relied on my head to steer me through life. But lately I was forced to acknowledge a yearning I couldn't quite name. I'm sure a therapist would ascribe this to a biological clock tick-tocking away in my empty uterus like the alarm clock inside the crocodile in Peter Pan. It was more complicated than that. Mostly, I was content with my single life, and proud of the independence I had achieved. I didn't want a child, and not just because I would be a terrible mother, bound to repeat the awful pattern of parenting I had experienced. And – I was less certain of this – I didn't want a partner. Yes, the regular sex would be nice, but sharing my space? I didn't think so. So why did I feel so overwhelmed by a few hours in bed with Dykstra? Maybe that atrophied muscle, my heart, struggled to assert itself at last? The only conclusion I reached was that I was too old for one-night stands, especially with Dykstra: they demanded more both physically and emotionally than I could cope with.

The Manhattan streets are never really empty; cabs, delivery vans and garbage trucks cruise through the night, and now the sidewalks far below also started to fill with people on their way to work. I needed to get to work too. I breathed a gusty sigh, turned away from the window and headed for the shower. Under its spray, I deliberately cleared my mind of Dykstra, and repopulated it with the various parties and lawyers whom I would meet in a few hours to start a second day of mediation.

Chapter 3

New York – Tuesday

I had told Dykstra that I didn't expect to see him again before he left for his book tour. Based on the lack of progress the day before, I envisaged another grueling day of arguments and posturing, leading nowhere. So I was pleasantly surprised when the lawyer representing the alleged trophy wife and gold-digger widow provided the breakthrough that led to a resolution before lunch.

Claudia Royce was a powerhouse in the same law firm I had slaved at in the late Nineties. She had joined the firm as a partner after I left, but I suspected she had agreed to my appointment to mediate this case because she thought the association gave her client an advantage. It didn't, but it did make me ponder whether, had I stuck the course, I might have been sitting in her chair, wearing her clothes and pulling in two million dollars a year. She had to be over fifty but looked forty, tall and slim, with skillfully cut and highlighted hair, discreet jewelry and very expensive, slightly mannish clothes. Her posture was perfect, her voice accentless. I had done my research on all the participants: she was a killer, a take-no-prisoners New York litigator with ice water in her veins.

At the end of the previous day's session, I had given the parties some homework: they were to think about a special time they had shared with the deceased. Why was it meaningful to them? What do they think it meant to their father/husband? Claudia refrained from the eye-rolling engaged in by the other lawyers – predictably, they were uncomfortable with anything that bypassed their role as advocates or smacked of emotion rather than argument – and I anticipated she would coach her client diligently in an appropriately heartfelt response.

The son, the firstborn, who had taken on the leadership of the family firm after his father's death, spoke first. Hesitantly, he described the cabin by a lake in New Hampshire where he and his sister had spent the summers as children.

"Do you remember the smell when we first opened it up in the spring?"

"The campfires?" His sister's eyes were shining. The day before she had barely said a word; now she was animated for the first time. Her lawyer squirmed in his seat.

After a few minutes of this exchange of memories, I noticed the widow's eyes misting over. I encouraged her to share what was on her mind, thinking that Claudia would jump in to protect her client from volunteering any vulnerability that might reduce her chances of winning the pot. Strangely, the lawyer was preoccupied under the table with her phone. I had asked everyone to turn off their cellphones at the start of the mediation the previous day, but had forgotten to repeat the request that morning. I was about to say something when Claudia stood up.

"I have to take this. It's my son-in-law. My daughter's in labor!"

She rushed out to the lobby, and I quickly called a break. Unlike the previous day, when a break in the proceedings signaled each faction's withdrawal to a corner of the conference room to whisper and cast venomous looks over their shoulders at the others, today everyone stayed seated, exchanging excited grins. Wonderful how the impending birth of a baby – even one so distantly connected as Claudia's soon-to-be grandchild – could alter the mood.

From then on, it was plain sailing, or what Sam would call "the magic of the process." By noon, the parties had worked out an agreement that gave each a share of the estate. I did little except cheer them on, and quietly send out for a bottle of champagne, so that when, at 12.13 p.m. precisely, Claudia's ecstatic son-in-law phoned with the news of an eight-pound three-ounce girl – "mother and baby doing fine" – we could celebrate the birth *and* the settlement appropriately.

I put my papers back into my briefcase, fished out my phone and turned it back on. A text from Dykstra: *Meeting Sam at Center at 2. Can you come?*

Yes, I could. I sprung for a cab from downtown to the hotel, sprinted inside to pack and check out, then grabbed another cab to Queens, expense be damned. Although the parties routinely reimburse the mediator's expenses without question, old habits die hard, and I usually took public transit whenever I could. I felt uncomfortable in taxis, watching the dollars and cents click upwards, calculating the tip, and wondering if the driver was taking me some roundabout route to drive up the fare; all due to a poverty-stricken youth, no doubt. However, this time euphoria swamped my miserly instincts: the settlement of the case, or the thought of seeing Dykstra again? I refused to second-guess myself, but leaned back against the cracked vinyl and breathed as shallowly as I could the cab's aggressively pine-scented air-freshener atmosphere, as we sliced and diced our way across Manhattan to the Queensboro Bridge.

We drew up at the Queens Dispute Resolution Center at two-thirty. A concrete bunker daubed in graffiti, the building had started life in the sixties as a warehouse and had undergone several re-purposings before it had been reborn to its current use.

"I love what you've done with the place," I said sarcastically, as I proffered a cheek to Sam who hurried up to meet me in the reception area, intercepting a large black woman who had risen to her feet and seemed ready to challenge my presence with her fists.

"It's OK, Shanya. She's here to see me." Sam held my arm as he guided me down a bleak corridor to his office. "Shanya's a volunteer, a little over-eager – a domestic abuse victim – but really a hard worker and sweet-natured when you get to know her. Yeah, I know, we could do with a new sofa and some artwork, but the grant-makers don't pay for frills. They want results, numbers .... "

"And you wonder why I don't want to go into the non-profit side of the business."

Sam smiled. I thought he seemed less haggard and tense than the evening before. Perhaps it was because he was so clearly in his element here, the mediation center he had developed from the ground up. In spite of its tawdry appearance, his program was a model for similar dispute resolution centers around the country. I imagined his work gave him some measure of comfort in his grief for Marta, or a distraction at least.

He opened the door to his office and ushered me in. Dykstra sat with his back to me, the afternoon sun making an aura around his head. He stood up, a mysterious silhouette until Sam lowered the blinds. As he came into focus, I felt a wave of optimism. Perhaps after all we *could* be friends – "friends with benefits" as the current cliché went. He had carved out time to help someone he did not know, just because I asked him to. Why was I so nervous around him? We exchanged a brief hug and murmured hellos. Sam glanced speculatively between us. Did he sense our very recent intimacy?

"Pieter's been really helpful, Sarah, and he has a plan. Pieter, why don't you explain."

"Well ...," Dykstra spoke hesitantly, looking at Sam for reassurance. This was uncharacteristic, and I wondered what the two of them had talked about before my arrival. Had Dykstra told Sam about our history? Surely not. I was, again, over-thinking things. Dykstra was here to give Sam some leads on finding his daughter, nothing more.

"I contacted an associate at *France-Soir,* he's a crime reporter and a stringer for Europ News. He gave me the name of a private investigator in Paris. My contact thinks the P.I. might take the case, but it would be very expensive, especially as we have so little to go on. Chantal is not even officially missing, so the police won't help. He told me that if we could give him three things it would make it much simpler to find her—and less expensive."

"So? What three things?"

"Chantal's cell phone number, her e-mail address and her car registration-- her license plate, as you call it here. From these, he thinks he can track her down in a matter of days. A credit card or her bank account number would also allow a trace of her movements, but that's harder to do, unless the police are involved, because of bank privacy rules …." His voice trailed off, avoiding something, I suspected.

"And the plan?"

Dykstra looked to Sam who responded.

"Pieter and I thought that the three of us, as soon as he's finished with his book tour, could go to France and find her cell phone number and the other things. Pieter speaks fluent French," – why was I not surprised? – "and Sarah, I'd really like you there when we find her. Your skills: you could mediate, explain, help me reconnect with Chantal ….."

"I don't know, Sam. My French is pretty rusty, for one thing. I understand that you're afraid she won't warm to you after all this time, but honestly I'm not sure that another American stranger is going to help much."

"But you're about her age, and I know you grew up without a father too. I just feel you could relate to her."

"That was different," I mumbled, and looked away. I had not shared the details of my childhood with Sam, or Dykstra either. I tried to avoid thinking about it. It was easier to believe my life started at eighteen when I arrived in the U.S. from London to take up a college scholarship at Rome College in North Georgia. Or at the earliest, when I was fourteen and fostered with Miss Mumford, the academic spinster who force-fed me education and researched my U.S. citizenship rights. For twenty-five years, my American father had been a presence only in my worst nightmares. The thought of him trying to reconnect with me in real life now made me shudder. I assumed he'd died; I hoped he had.

The silence grew uncomfortably long. Both men looked at me questioningly.

"Anyway, I have a practice to run. I can't just fly off to France." Unspoken, but also on my mind, was the cost of the enterprise. A plane ticket to Paris might cost a thousand dollars in high season, as well as expenses while there. I was self-employed and my income was unpredictable. I liked to keep a healthy reserve in savings, and this could take a big bite out of that. "Socially liberal, fiscally conservative," that was me.

"Didn't you tell me that once this New York case settled you had nothing on your plate except for preparing for the law school course you're teaching fall semester?" Sam reminded me gently.

I sighed.

"Look, let me think about it. When will your book tour be over?"

"The eighteenth." Dykstra looked at his watch. "Oh God, speaking of which, I'm supposed to be at the Greenlight Bookstore in Brooklyn at five-thirty. I'd better get going."

Sam and I walked him back to the reception area where dragon-lady Shanya was gathering her things together in preparation for closing up shop. Dykstra gave me a long hug.

"Please, do think about coming to France. It could be fun," He whispered in my ear, the warmth of his breath evoking body memories of last night's lovemaking.

"The last time you invited me for a 'fun trip,' we both nearly died," I whispered back, then pushed him firmly away. "Have a great time, and sell lots of books."

Sam and I stood together in the darkened lobby for a few more minutes, reminiscing about the old days, until my cab arrived.

"Sarah, I do hope you'll come to France with me. I'll pay your way. Marta left me a load of money she inherited from her parents, and you know we never lived extravagantly. She would want me to spend the money on this, I'm sure."

"That's generous, but I'm still not sure I can be helpful. I will think about it, though."

I felt better about saying goodbye to him this time: he seemed invigorated by Dykstra's visit, and by the plan they had created together to find Chantal. I was not as worried as him about her reaction after they found her, but then I knew what a sweetheart he was.

***

La Guardia was a madhouse at six p.m. on a Thursday with business people eager to get home before the weekend rush. I groaned out loud when I located my flight on the Departures screen: delayed to eight-thirty. I decided not to check my roll-on bag in case I could squeeze onto an earlier departure, and muscled my way through to the security line, and then to the gate that serviced the Delta shuttle to Atlanta.

The gate area was crammed with passengers bumped from other flights. The incoming plane had been delayed by weather conditions in Atlanta. According to CNN, more than a dozen tornadoes had touched down in Mississippi and Alabama, and the storm was heading northeast. I managed to find myself a seat and plugged in my laptop, determined to immerse myself in the follow-up from the mediation, and block out the surrounding chaos.

I have a gift, I guess. My ability to focus exclusively on the task at hand served me well in my education and career, but it has a social downside: people tend to think I'm aloof, even unfriendly. I can certainly be attentive to the personalities in a mediation setting; after all, that's my livelihood. However, I've nurtured my independence for so long that the casual niceties that come easily to others – for example, my fellow-travelers chatting to each other about the flight delays – were hard for me. So I worked on reviewing documents and crafting e-mails, tying up all the loose ends that I would have normally attended to in my home office the next day.

"Fuck!" The explosion from my seat-mate penetrated my cone of concentration. I looked up to see that the flight information on the overhead TV screens had changed: "Delayed" was replaced by "Cancelled." At the same moment, the Delta agent, barely audible over the disgusted groans and complaints of the crowd in the gate area, announced that "due to continued bad weather in the area, the Atlanta airport has been closed, and all incoming flights are cancelled for the evening."

Quick work on the internet snagged me the last available room at the airport Marriott Courtyard, and, an hour later, I phoned the front desk for a wake-up call at five-thirty a.m. so that I could catch the first flight out. I had barely slept the night before, and hadn't eaten much. The adrenalin that had kept me moving forward through a very long day was rapidly draining away. I think I was asleep before I hung up the phone.

Chapter 4

Decatur – Wednesday

The storms of the night before had swept the sky clear. At ten a.m., I landed in Atlanta under a cloudless blue dome. The temperature was – unusual for June – a degree or two cooler than New York, and with less humidity. It was good to be home, and to anticipate some downtime to think about Sam's situation, and my renewed connection to Dykstra.

My first inkling that all was not well came when I left the MARTA station for the ten minute walk to my house. Downed branches and leaves still cluttered the sidewalk, although the roadway had been cleared. The rise-and-fall of a chainsaw's whine greeted me as I turned onto my street. A neighbor, with whom I had previously only exchanged nods, stood up from gathering tree debris in his front yard, and hailed me.

"Everything OK over there?" He jerked his head towards my place across and down the street. I realized with a feeling of sinking dread that the chainsaw noise was coming from my place. Now I could see a truck pulled up in my driveway, one I thought I recognized.

"I don't know," I muttered, and hurried across the street, my roll-on case bouncing down the curb, dragging a train of twigs.

Yes, it *was* Gerardo's truck. Gerardo was my handyman, although that title doesn't reflect our relationship as it has developed over the years. I first enlisted his help while I was in the throes of rehabilitating my hundred-year-old Craftsman bungalow, the only place I could afford when I returned to Atlanta to start my mediation practice. I wanted to do as much of the work myself as I could, not just because of financial necessity, but also because of a need to sublimate the excess emotion and energy which kept me fizzing and twitching during those first slow and doubtful years. However, there were many jobs that needed two people to complete, one of whom needed to be bigger and stronger than me. Gerardo was not a licensed contractor, but he had a wealth of knowledge picked up in under-the-table construction work, he was reliable, and a hard worker. We worked well together, most often in silence punctuated only by grunts of effort or monosyllabic instructions. Even though I had never been invited to his house, and didn't expect to be in the future, I thought of him as my friend. What he thought of me, he kept to himself.

I edged around his truck, and rounded the rear corner of the house. I couldn't recognize any element of the chaos confronting me. Shock doubled me over like a punch to the stomach. A wall of tangled branches rose up fifteen feet, blocking the space between the house and the detached garage at the back of the lot. The venerable water oak tree that stood in the middle of the back yard had fallen. The tree must have been planted at the same time the house was built a hundred years ago by a thoughtful gardener anticipating the future when it would shade the house from the brutal summer sun, as well as providing scale and beauty to the utilitarian residential landscape. I had sat under its spreading branches many times, but now I was seeing it from a new angle: yesterday, this would have been a bird's eye view.

"Gerardo!" I yelled, but he couldn't hear me over the roar of the saw's motor. I could barely see him on the other side of the leafy morass, and I could do nothing but wait until the crash of a severed branch signaled a respite. In the ringing silence that followed, my repeated shout sounded hoarse and a little hysterical.

"Sarah? I meet you at front, okay?"

"Okay." I retraced my steps around his truck and reclaimed the luggage I had abandoned in the driveway. Gerardo emerged from the other side of the house and we met at the porch steps.

"How bad is it? Is the house damaged? I couldn't see anything." A look at his face disabused me of the hope that by some miracle the tree had fallen neatly between the two structures without harming either. He had left the chainsaw at the back of the house and pulled his protective goggles down round his neck, but was still wearing big leather gauntlets.

"*Si*, but maybe not so bad. We go inside, yes? I cut—" Here, he mimed sawing actions, "But not yet to the door at back."

I fumbled in my purse for the front door key, still in denial that anything truly catastrophic could have happened to my beloved bungalow. At first glance, the main room seemed unchanged from when I had locked the front door behind me several days ago. Then I became conscious of the different way the light fell on the furniture. Instead of being illuminated from the windows at the front and right side of the room, daylight was spilling in from the left side where my bedroom, office and the bathroom were located. I walked to the arch separating that side of the house from the living room, and turned to the back of the house, towards my open bedroom door. I remembered pulling down the blinds on the bedroom windows before I left to keep the place cool in my absence. The blinds were gone. So was the window, the one that had a view of the back yard with the majestic oak tree in the center. Instead, there was a gaping hole that stretched up to the roof, exposing through the rafters the clear blue sky that had cheered me only an hour ago. Debris filled the room: pieces of the roof structure, broken glass and sheetrock, leaves and branches, including one thicker limb that had evidently done most of the damage. In amongst the chaos remained strange little vignettes of the comfortable retreat that had previously existed: a bedside lamp with a milk-glass shade, and beside it, the library book I had been reading, a grocery store receipt marking the place I had left off.

Random thoughts flashed through my mind. When was that library book due back? Had I made the bed before I left? I couldn't remember and I couldn't tell now; it was covered with wreckage. Suddenly, I found it difficult to catch my breath, and my shoulders started shaking.

"Is OK, Sarah. We can fix it," Gerardo took my arm and tried to lead me back to the living room. I jerked away.

"It's *not* OK! My home has been destroyed!" I gulped back sobs, clenching my fists with a sudden urge to hit out at something, anything.

Gerardo's voice became stern.

"*Si*. Is OK. Is just …" He searched for the English word, "… furniture." He pointed to the remains of the bed which I had positioned so that my view on waking would be the back yard. "Sarah, if you are *en casa,* in the bed, you…." Here he made the universal gesture for death, drawing his fingers across his throat. "But you are not *en casa* and you are alive."

I stared at him while his words sank in. I felt my panicky rage ebbing away, and I took a deep shuddering breath.

"I'm sorry, Gerardo. You're right. It's just so ….." I took another look at the damage before turning away. "Thank you so much for being here, but how did you know?"

"Bad storm. I drive by early to check."

Yes, he was indeed my friend.

***

The rest of the day spun by in a blur of activity. I called the insurance company first, and then worked my way down the list of approved contractors the adjuster gave me. It quickly became evident I was not the only Atlanta homeowner with property damage from the storm. I eventually managed to schedule three appointments to get competing estimates for repairs, although each contractor warned me it might be weeks before they could actually get round to doing the work. I *was* able to arrange for a dumpster to be delivered, and Gerardo started to fill it with debris. With his help, I also managed to work my way to the walk-in closet, and extract jeans, T-shirt and sneakers, more practical clothes for the tasks at hand. It was surreal to stand in the wreckage of my bedroom and open the closet door on untouched ranks of dresses, suits and shirts, all my treasured high-heeled shoes standing neatly at attention in the rack I had built for them.

Neighbors came by with sandwiches and iced tea to commiserate and offer help. One couple, whose names I learned for the first time were Debbie and John Olsen, even offered to have me to stay at their place while the rebuilding was in progress. I found myself blinking away tears; I was touched by their generosity. John was a meteorologist with the Weather Channel, and Deb was a middle school science teacher. They had no children, hence the spare bedroom. The man who had first alerted me to trouble as I walked home that morning arrived. Perry Dexter turned out to be a single dad with two teenage girls.

"They're driving me crazy," he claimed, before proudly reciting all their achievements in athletics. "Come over for dinner tomorrow. I'd like you to tell them about your career. They need a role model."

I chided myself for the cynicism with which I had in the past lumped these people together as yuppies, social climbers who defined themselves by the make of German car they drove. I hadn't taken the time to get to know any of them, but here they were, ready to pitch in and help me.

Late in the afternoon, Gerardo and I made a run to Home Depot for tarpaulins and plywood sheets. By then, he had cut up and stacked the main limbs, clearing paths around the house to the back door and to the garage. The tree trunk itself would need more work. We also removed most of the mess from the bedroom, and pulled out the few salvageable items. It was eight o'clock and the light was fading when we finally finished securing blue tarps over the six-foot-wide gash in the roof and nailing plywood over the hole in the back wall. Gerardo shrugged off my repeated thanks, pocketed the check I pressed on him without looking at it, and roared off in a cloud of exhaust smoke.

I poured myself a glass of red wine and cut a slab of the lasagna someone had dropped off. I contemplated heating it up, then decided I might fall asleep before it was done, so I ate it cold standing at the kitchen counter. I stripped off my dirty work clothes, and crawled into the nest I made on the couch from a spare duvet. I expected to drop immediately into unconsciousness as I had done the night before, but instead I lay there thinking how lucky I was. I was alive, I had insurance, and now I had neighbors whose names I knew and who I could count on for help. Most of all, I had a friend, Gerardo, who looked out for me.

Since coming home, I had not thought once of Dykstra, or Sam, or the request that I go to France with them. Now, as I was counting my blessings, I realized I needed to include them in the list. I was drifting in that pleasant space between sleep and wakefulness when it hit me with the force of a lightning bolt. I *would* go to France. Once I had squared away a contractor, there was nothing useful I could do in Decatur, and camping out in my broken house while I waited for the builders to start would be frustrating, if not depressing. I wouldn't wait for Dykstra's book tour to finish. Instead, I would use the time before work started on the house to winkle out the details the French private investigator needed, so that, by the time Sam and Dykstra arrived in Dordogne in two weeks, I could present the information to them and foreshorten the search for Chantal. It would be my gift to Sam, in return for the friendship he had given me, and also a way to pay forward all the kindness I had been shown today. I was awake again, and eager to do something to translate my idea into action. I retrieved my cell phone and tapped in an email:

Sam: Yes, I'll go to France. Will call tomorrow with details. Love, Sarah

Now I could rest.

Chapter 5

France – Monday

  I studied French for five years at Clapham Abbey, the all-girls private high school in London that I attended on a scholarship secured by Margaret Mumford who taught English there. Thanks to the rigorous drilling I received, by the time I sat for the "A" level exam in the subject, I could not only quote at length from Racine and Molière, I could also correctly use the subjunctive voice in regular and irregular verbs, both transitive and intransitive. Of more practical use were the two miserable summers I spent on school-sponsored "exchanges" with French families. As I had no family of my own to reciprocate with hospitality to a French girl, the first summer – I was sixteen – I found myself shoe-horned in with another Clapham Abbey girl's host family who lived near Rouen in Normandy. *Trois* turned out to be a crowd, and I spent most of that summer with the French exchange student's obnoxious younger brother. Between dropping worms down the back of my dress and leaving spiders in my bed, he taught me all the dirty words and insults he knew.

  The following summer, the school foisted me on a childless older couple who thought it would be *trés amusant* to have a young English person in the household. Under the guise of teaching me French domestic customs, they treated me as a maid. I resented all the fetching and carrying, laying and clearing of tables, and dusting of bibelots that cluttered their elegant townhouse in a western suburb of Paris. However, I made the most of my substantial free time while

Monsieur and Madame were attending social events to which I was emphatically not invited. I took the *métro* into the city and roamed for hours, often ending up at *les Deux Magots*, a sidewalk café in the heart of the Left Bank on the Boulevard St. Germain. I made one cup of coffee last for hours as I imagined myself back into the Twenties, rubbing shoulders with Picasso and Gertrude Stein, or the Fifties, arguing philosophy and politics with Jean-Paul Sartre. Strangely, I had not spared a thought then about the Sixties, when Sam and his fellow students had been here plotting revolution, perhaps sitting on the same cane-backed chairs under the scornful gaze of the same saturnine waiter.

This would be my third time in France. As the plane taxied towards the terminal at Charles de Gaulle Airport, I wondered whether the colloquialisms I learned during those summers would come back to me, and if they did, whether they would be hopelessly dated more than two decades on. I had slept for a little over two hours on the flight from Atlanta. I hoped it would be enough to keep me alert as I navigated my way through customs and immigration, and found the bus to take me into Paris. I was cutting it fine if I was to make my reserved seat on the TGV (*train de grande vitesse*) to Angoulême from the Montparnasse station. I was grateful I had only packed a carry-on bag.

The bus was crowded with excited students making the twenty-first century equivalent of the Grand Tour. Their loud voices and immense backpacks marked them as Americans. They evinced an almost motherly reaction from me: I wanted to smooth their tousled hair and tell them to watch out for pickpockets. However, I suppressed those urges and turned towards the window, eager for my first sight of the Paris skyline. Once we left the autoroute, the traffic thickened, and I kept glancing at my watch calculating the slim margin of time left to make my transfer. When the bus swung into the terminus, there was no opportunity for more than a glimpse of the Eiffel Tower between the new office blocks that had sprung up since my last visit. I promised myself a whole day in the city on the way home, then hurried inside the station.

It was noon, French time, on a cool, grey day, the fifth since I had arrived home to find my bedroom uninhabitable, and had taken the decision to search solo for Chantal Dubenoit, Sam's missing daughter. Sinking gratefully into my assigned seat on the TGV, I mentally reviewed the information Sam had given me. The details were all carefully noted on my laptop stowed in the overhead rack, but I didn't need to refer to them. I could still hear Sam's voice as he described the farmhouse where Chantal lived, the old woman next door, and St. Barthélemy, the market town five kilometers away. I had reserved a room in the same small hotel he had stayed in back in April. Clearly, the farmhouse was the place to start, but if, like him, I found no traces there to follow, I had her Limoges address as well, the apartment where she had lived with her mother Claire, until Claire's death the year before.

I had spoken to Sam by phone several times in the last days, in between wrangling insurance adjusters and building contractors. Sam was elated that I had decided to go to France, but a little worried when I told him I wanted to go alone in advance of him and Dykstra. After some discussion, I agreed to let him pay for the airplane fare and reimburse me later for a rental car and hotel room. I'd cover my food and any incidental expenses. I'd heard great things about French country cuisine, and didn't want my menu choices to be constrained by guilt that Sam was picking up the tab.

"You will keep in touch, Sarah? E-mail me anything you find, won't you?" Time differences and expense would make cell phone calls a less preferable means of communication.

Dykstra opposed my plan. Our one conversation was rushed and unsatisfactory, interrupted by a strident female voice – his agent? – telling him to "hurry up!" I couldn't tell if he was pouting because he felt cheated out of "a fun trip" with me, or because he genuinely doubted my ability to unearth the information needed to locate Chantal. Either way,

I resolved not to care. He and Sam were arriving in Dordogne seven days after me. I would deal with Dykstra in person then. In the meantime, I would copy him diligently on my e-mail reports to Sam. Although loopy with jetlag, I was excited to be in France again and engaged in an adventure. I had a good feeling that I'd secure the leads necessary to nail down Chantal's location. I have to admit to an element of "I'll show 'em" smugness too. I could already picture Dykstra's face when I presented the information; he wasn't the only one who could track down a story.

Soon we escaped the dingy southern suburbs. Reflecting my mood, the sun came out. Angoulême was about three hundred miles southwest of Paris, and about fifty miles west of Limoges where Chantal had grown up. The two cities stood like guardians on the northern edge of the lush rural region of Dordogne. There were no cities of comparable size within Dordogne; just market towns and villages serving the farming community and the increasing number of British expatriates who made their home there.

As the train passed smoothly and almost noiselessly through green and gold countryside, I pondered Chantal's life. It was unusual for a child to continue to live as an adult with a parent until that parent's death, even in these straitened economic times. Perhaps Chantal had some disability, or was emotionally fragile like Laura, the daughter in Tennessee Williams' play, *A Glass Menagerie.* Or maybe the problem was with a mother who clung obsessively to her only child, imprisoning her with love and guilt, its evil twin. I thought about the damage the years might have wrought on Chantal. Would Sam ever be able to reclaim her as his daughter, redeem those lost years and establish a "normal" relationship? For the first time, I understood his request that I mediate their mutual reconnection. He might have exaggerated my inter-personal skills, but it would be valuable to have a neutral third person present as a buffer.

I closed my eyes against the brightness streaming through the window. The next thing I knew the doors were hissing shut as the train prepared to pull out of Poitiers. Next stop, Angoulême. My confidence suffered a slight knock at the Hertz kiosk at Angouleme station. I could have sworn I'd specified an automatic transmission when I booked the rental car, but the agent, who spoke irritatingly perfect English, thus robbing me of my chance to try out my language skills, gave a Gallic shrug: the only available vehicle in the tiny lot was manual shift, take it or leave it. I took it, and spent the first five minutes alternately doing bunny hops and stalling, as I relearned the depress-clutch, change-gear, release-clutch routine. By the time I was clear of the town and headed south-east on the D 939, I mastered the technique and my driving smoothed out, although still clearly not fast enough for other drivers, who stuck close to my tail until a blind curve or the approaching summit of a hill provided them an opportunity to attempt suicide-by-passing.

After crossing the little river that marked the border between the Charente department and Dordogne, I pulled over to consult the Google Maps printout I brought with me from Atlanta. From then on, I followed minor roads through wooded hills and meadows, where large white cows stared stupidly over hedgerows. Grey stone villages, named for obscure saints, slumbered in the warmth of the June afternoon. There was little traffic. The vacation season had not yet started in earnest. In July and August, even this rural region would be crowded with Parisians fleeing to their *maisons secondaires* and northern Europeans seeking an authentic French country experience.

I found St. Barthélemy-en-Bussac without difficulty and parked in the main square to get my bearings. The square was actually an irregularly-shaped cobbled space in front of a church – dedicated to St. Barthélemy, no doubt – whose spire leaned protectively over the ancient buildings huddled below. Several narrow streets led from the square at odd angles, including the one I had taken from the main road that by-passed the town.

Sam had recommended the Hotel Montbrun, the only hotel in the town, on rue du Presbytère, which I correctly surmised ran next to the church. The lobby was dark and cool, smelling faintly of lavender, with wood-paneled walls, well-polished furniture, and a red-tiled floor. An older gentleman with a military moustache emerged from a room on the left, and I finally had a chance to try out my French.

"*Bonjour, Monsieur.* My name is Sarah McKinney. I have reserved a room."

"*Bien sûr, Madame.*" I suspected I was the only guest scheduled to arrive that day, as he had no need to consult the leather-bound register – no computer screen here – which lay open on an antique writing desk. I concentrated on following his rapid French, as he welcomed me to the Hotel Montbrun, apologized for the fact that the elevator was broken, and explained the arrangements for breakfast: the hotel had no restaurant but I could take my *petit-déjeuner* in the lobby, or on the terrace if I preferred. Then he gripped my bag and preceded me up the stairs to my room on the second floor back with a view over the terrace to a pretty walled garden. After assuring me I could leave my car parked in front of the church, he left me to settle in.

I liked the charming simplicity of the room, with its ancient and massive armoire and carved headboard. As I sat gingerly down on the edge of the bed, I was relieved to find that the mattress was more modern. The bed linens were sparkling white and crisp; the duvet invitingly plump. I walked into the bathroom, and nearly fell headlong into the shower. It was the smallest room I had ever seen, but still managed to accommodate a sink, toilet and bidet, although to use the latter, I would have to sit with my feet in the shower stall. I unpacked, washed my face and took off my shoes. It was almost five o'clock. I decided on an hour's nap, then a stroll before dinner. I felt sure no self-respecting French village could survive without a restaurant or two, and I expected my host would point me in the right direction. I would start my inquiries the next morning after overcoming the worst of my jetlag.

Strangely, as soon as I lay down on top of the deliciously puffy duvet, any possibility of sleep vanished. My brain was humming like a race car waiting for the flag to drop. I wanted to get started. Several hours of daylight remained, and restaurants wouldn't start serving dinner until eight anyway. The reverberations of the church bell tolling five o'clock made up my mind; there would probably be a similar racket at the quarter and half hour too: who could sleep through that?

I stripped, managed to bang both elbows painfully against the tiles in my attempt to take a quick shower, then dressed again in some crumpled linen pants and a fitted white tee-shirt. Leaving off the make-up and pulling my damp hair into a ponytail felt freeing. After all, I knew no one here and had no professional image to maintain. I emerged into the evening sunlight with a clean and shiny face, feeling just like the teenager I had been the last time I was in France.

Chapter 6

France - Monday

The road to Chantal's last known address meandered lazily along a valley lined with market gardens, "*fermettes*" in the local jargon. I drove slowly, eyes peeled for the finger post announcing the turn to Le Bec, the name of the former farm complex which had been subdivided many years before to create two homes. Sam had told me that the land itself and associated outbuildings were rented out to local farmers. I nearly passed the lane, a narrow gravel trail, lined with untended trees bending over to form a tunnel of deep shade. The lane sloped upwards for a quarter mile before breaking into the open. Fields planted with cheerful yellow rapeseed extended on either side. I continued uphill past an ancient stone barn on the right, and then drove into a stand of pines which announced the farmhouse itself. I pulled the car up on a stretch of weedy stones, and sat for a moment, taking in the scene.

   The long, two-story farmhouse was constructed of honey-colored stone, different from the grey flintier material that I had seen in the villages and in St. Barthélemy. A tall wooden barn, its wide doors open to reveal a black rectangle of emptiness, formed an angle to the building. Originally, one extended family must have occupied Le Bec and worked the surrounding land, all their needs met in the sprawling complex: bakery, laundry, dairy, as well as a shelter for animals and the primitive agricultural machinery probably still in use as recently as fifty years ago.

Obviously, there were now two dwellings. On the right, a newish-looking door with a glass panel had been inserted into the wall between closely-shuttered windows. Unkempt lavender bushes flanked this door, but otherwise no attempt had been made to prettify the façade. On the left side of the building, a climbing rose with white blooms the size of small cabbages arched over what looked like the original entrance: a heavy oak door with iron studs and hinges. On this side, the shutters were painted blue, and, though latched together, were angled slightly outwards to allow some light to penetrate inside. White-painted stones encircled a herb garden situated within handy reach of the door, its greenery interspersed with bright orange marigolds. The cheerful residence where I hoped to find the first leads in my search contrasted clearly with the unoccupied, slightly forbidding half which must be Chantal's.

I approached the oak door, mentally rehearsing the French phrases to explain my presence. I raised my hand to knock, then noticed that the door was a few inches ajar, probably to facilitate some air-flow. Behind it, a shadowy corridor led towards the back of the house, and I could hear kitchen noises – water running and pans being moved. I let my hand fall onto the wood, and then, suspecting that no one had heard the rap, I called out.

"Bonsoir, Madame?"

A water tap shut off and steps approached. I prepared my friendliest smile, as the door opened further to reveal—a man, thirty-ish, slim, not tall, thick black hair and a neat beard, dark brown eyes made more intense by the well-defined lateral lines of his eyebrows, an aquiline nose. He was dressed in a white undershirt and khaki shorts. His feet were bare.

Having assumed I would meet an elderly woman, my prepared speech turned to pebbles in my mouth. The man looked at me inquiringly.

"Bonsoir. Puis-je vous aider?"

I managed to stutter out my name, that I was looking for Chantal Dubenoit; I was a friend of her father's.

"You are American? …English?" I was split between relief that I would not after all have to struggle on in French, and chagrin that he had picked me out for a foreigner so easily. Was my accent that bad? He continued, "Mademoiselle Dubenoit owns the house next door, but I do not think she has been here for many months." His English was virtually accentless, with just an attractive softening of the s and th sounds into z's. I thought briefly of Dykstra. His English was perfect, but more clipped, more sibilant than this man's.

"Er, yes. Her father was here looking for her in April. He spoke to a lady living here who knew her and who could perhaps help me to find her."

"My mother."

Yes! Now we were getting somewhere.

"Is she here? May I speak to her?"

He paused, his compelling eyes not leaving mine.

"My mother is dead. She died last month. That is why I am here, to …. make arrangements. I don't know where Mademoiselle Dubenoit is."

I felt my whole body slump with disappointment. The old lady was my best lead. The sense of optimism that had buoyed me up since the plane landed in Paris ten hours previously, drained away in a second, leaving me depleted.

"I'm so sorry for your loss." The words were rote, a knee-jerk formula of social nicety, but, whether he mistook my dejection as evidence of sincere sympathy, or he realized that my sadness was purely selfish, he extended his hand to me.

"My name is Pierre Albert. Please come through to the garden, and sit for a while. Perhaps we can figure something out."

As I followed him down the corridor, I remembered the stranger Sam had found in Chantal's house, the man who had rushed away before Sam could question him. He had dark hair too, but long enough for a ponytail. Sam hadn't mentioned a beard. That was over two months ago: hair could be cut, beards grown. I dismissed the thought that Pierre Albert could be the same man. That encounter had seemed sinister; this guy was friendly and direct. Good-looking, too.

The corridor led to a small utilitarian kitchen, appliances that looked forty years old, worn Formica countertops, and an open door onto a terrace of terra cotta tiles. The man led me through it, indicated a café table and two chairs under a grape arbor at one end, then retreated into the kitchen. I sat down, noticing how the black coating on the furniture had blistered to reveal patches of rusty metal underneath. Flower pots in varying sizes lined the edge of the terrace. Some were planted with more herbs, others with geraniums, the blooms forming impressionistic dabs of pink and red. At six o'clock, the sun was declining into the west but its heat was still strong. Grateful for the dappled shade of the arbor, I closed my eyes and breathed in the light aroma of the vine above already burdened with cascades of tiny green grapes. I was grateful too for the chance to regroup. Perhaps I should have waited to begin the investigation until tomorrow after all. Maybe jetlag was exaggerating my reactions. I took a deep breath and stretched my legs out. All was not lost. I just had to switch to Plan B, whatever Plan B was.

Pierre came out carrying a bottle of Evian, condensation already beading it, and a tall glass. He had put on a collared shirt and sandals. He poured the water, and sat down in the other chair.

"Your English is perfect. What is it that you do?"

Silence. I cursed myself for my stupidity. In the States, asking someone what they do is a standard conversation opener. In Europe, people are more reserved. They do not relish revealing personal information on a first meeting. I knew that, for goodness' sake! As I considered how to redeem my ineptness, Pierre spoke.

"I have been working for five years with First Nations people in Canada, in the west, Yukon Territory. That is why I speak English." After a pause, he added quietly, "I am a priest."

Now I was thoroughly discomfited. Possible responses – *Wow, you don't look like a priest* – spun through my head, while I stared gormlessly at him. But priests could be young and good-looking, I supposed, and off duty, they could dress however they liked. Should I call him 'Père Pierre' now? Or 'Father Albert?' A hysterical giggle threatened to explode in my throat. I compressed my lips and looked down at my lap. I needed to pull myself together, and start behaving like a grown-up. The best remedy was to revert to the reason I was there in the first place.

"Do you know Chantal? Can you tell me anything that might help me locate her?"

"I have not seen her for many years, not since I was a child. After my father died, my mother was forced to divide the house, and rent out the land. Chantal's grandfather bought that part," Pierre indicated the shut-up half of the farmhouse, "as a *maison secondaire*, a country house for the summer vacations. He was a dentist, I believe, in Limoges. Chantal and her mother came for a couple of weeks every August. The grandparents died, and then Chantal and her mother didn't come here anymore—I was in seminary by this time. The house was closed down. My mother had a key and went in occasionally to make sure everything was all right, but no one lived there until Chantal moved in last winter."

"What was she like? Sam, my friend, hasn't met her since she was about eleven. I don't even know what she looks like."

He paused, his head tilted to one side as he tried to put his memories into words.

"I was a kid, and she seemed already grown-up, maybe eighteen, twenty. Quiet, serious. She stayed inside with her mother. I think her mother didn't like the sun, or maybe she had allergies, I can't remember. The old man, Chantal's grandfather, he was a bit of a snob. He pretended to be the ... lord? The master of the estate? He wore tweeds, wanted to hunt, but the local people didn't like him, wouldn't go shooting with him. My mother said he was a bully, told me to stay away, so I never really talked to Chantal or her mother. She was very beautiful......"

"Chantal?"

"No, her mother. Very beautiful: black hair, pale skin, tall and slim, lovely deep voice. Chantal's hair was mouse brown. In fact, next to her mother, she *was* a mouse." He sighed. "It's long ago, hard to remember."

"Your mother told you about Chantal, I mean, after she returned?"

"Yes, we spoke by phone at Christmas. She told me Chantal's mother was dead, and Chantal was living here. She was sorry for her; she thought she could help her." He smiled. "My mother was old-fashioned. She didn't like the telephone. But she wrote to me, every two weeks, whether I responded or not. After the Christmas phone call, I received regular reports on Chantal: my mother took her to mass, to bingo, to take tea with her friends in the area. She said Chantal seemed ... *désinteressée* ...   not interested. What a surprise! My mother and her friends were old women, thirty years older at least.

"In February, my mother became concerned, then, in March, worried: 'Chantal is not happy; she shuts herself up in the house, she will not go to mass.' My mother called the local curé – the parish priest. He came to visit Chantal, but he would not tell Mother what they talked about. Then – pouf! – Chantal disappears! I received that letter in April, perhaps the same time your friend was here. I did not receive another letter."

We sat in silence, gazing out over the patchy lawn – more weeds than grass – to a line of trees that delineated the border between the garden and the farmland beyond. The sun was just beginning to dip below the tree-tops; doves called softly to each other. I sipped my water, and tried to organize the questions that circled my brain. Had Chantal tired of the country life and headed back to Limoges? Did the parish curé hold the key to her discontent? If so, I doubted he'd tell me about it, if he'd refused to share it with his long-time parishioner, Pierre's mother. My best bet was to go to

Limoges, to Chantal's old address, and see if I could learn anything there about her recent movements. I felt lethargic and reluctant to move, but there seemed little more I could ask the young priest.

"Well, I think—" Together, we rose out of our chairs.

"Would you like to see inside Chantal's house? I still have the key."

I had forgotten the second purpose in coming here. After interviewing the old woman, I had planned to ask for a tour to see if Sam had missed any clues when he surveyed Chantal's deserted home. I hesitated. Now that I was actually here, to enter uninvited seemed an invasion of privacy. Chantal was finally becoming real to me, and the parallels between her life and mine – her age, gender and absentee father – which I had noted objectively before, now engendered a feeling of sympathy. How would *I* feel if strangers tramped through my house, opening drawers, fingering my things? But what was the point of coming to France if I wasn't prepared to gather all the information I could? I pushed my scruples aside.

"Yes, that would be helpful, thank you. Are you sure you don't mind?"

"It's no problem."

I followed him back into the kitchen. As he hunted through a drawer for the key, I noticed the vegetables on the counter top.

"But I'm interrupting your dinner preparations. I could come back another time."

"It's no problem," he repeated. "It's too early for dinner." He smiled and held up a key. "Here it is!"

The moment he smiled, I made the connection: Pierre … Peter …. Pieter … Dykstra! Some cosmic jokester was playing games with me while I was disoriented from sleep deprivation. Apparently I was fated to meet attractive men with some variation of the same name until … what? I succumbed? But this Pierre/Pieter was a priest, presumably Catholic, presumably celibate, presumably unavailable, and so the name was just a coincidence. For the third time since I arrived at the farmhouse, I took a deep breath and resolved to focus on the task at hand.

Chapter 7

France - Monday

Dust motes danced in a shaft of light from the open front door. The atmosphere in Chantal's house felt thick, like a crypt unsealed after centuries, although this air had rested undisturbed for no more than a couple of months. The place didn't smell bad though, just a little stale. I advanced carefully to the center of the room which seemed to combine both living and dining functions. Behind me, Pierre fumbled for the light switch, and the furniture leapt into life like a stage set: Act One, enter the stranger.

"Interesting. The electricity is still connected."

I turned to him with an inquiring look.

"Electricity in France is very expensive. When one leaves for a long time, one cuts it off at the main switch."

"Hmm." I surveyed the room. To my right, a sofa and two armchairs covered in bland beige tweed flanked an enormous stone fireplace with an opening large enough to spit-roast a pig, obviously part of the original structure before conversion into two dwellings. On my left was a pine dining table and four upright chairs, all varnished in an ugly yellowish color. A dresser with the same taffy-like finish stood against the wall. If I had to guess, the furniture had been purchased sometime in the Seventies with an eye to economy rather than style. There was no artwork on the walls, and none of the ornaments, books or other everyday jumble of a lived-in house.

"What are you looking for?" Pierre asked.

"Bank statements, phone bills, correspondence; anything that might be a clue to her life, and to where she might be now." My eyes alighted on the dresser drawers. I fought a quick battle with my better self, the self that was reluctant to pry into someone else's personal papers, and approached. But the drawers and the side cupboards contained nothing but silverware, table linens and a variety of cheap glasses.

"Come see this." Pierre had gone into the adjoining kitchen, and was leaning over the open door of a small refrigerator. I looked over his shoulder. The fridge contained a few cartons of yogurt, some packaged cheeses, bottled water and an assortment of jams and condiments. No meat or fresh produce. I picked up one of the yogurts. On the foil top: *'à consommer avant 24/4/11'* – consume before April 24, 2011.

"They're all the same: expired." Pierre closed the refrigerator door.

"It looks like she didn't plan on being away so long. Perhaps she's fallen ill, or had an accident—"

"Or she's enjoying herself so much wherever she is, she's decided to stay there longer." Pierre was evidently the glass-half-full type. I was glad he hadn't merely unlocked the door and left me to it, but had come inside with me. I wanted him there as a witness, and, in spite of his years away, his local knowledge meant he would pick up on things I missed, like the still-connected electricity. Besides all that, I instinctively liked him; he seemed honest and unaffected. Perhaps because he was a priest, I felt safe with him, although I had known him for all of half an hour. The priest thing was intriguing too; I wanted to ask him a dozen questions, but I knew better than to risk our very new companionship by posing them.

The kitchen held no other clues. An upper cupboard revealed canned food, pasta and rice; a lower one, some battered pots and pans. Drawers contained the expected ensemble of kitchen utensils, the trashcan was empty, and the countertops were clean and bare. The small range looked to be the same ancient vintage as the refrigerator; I couldn't see any small appliances. Chantal seemed not to have imported any modern kitchen conveniences during her short residence: no coffee-maker or blender, or even a cheerful dish towel or pretty calendar. The place probably remained exactly as it was when her grandparents used it as a summer home twenty-five years ago.

We went back to the main room, and Pierre led the way through another internal door which opened onto a short hallway leading to the stairs with a bathroom on the right. Again, the impersonal appearance struck me: the porcelain was dull with age, but clean; the well-worn white towels were symmetrically arranged. I found a package of over-the-counter painkillers in the medicine cabinet, along with a toothbrush still in its wrapping, toothpaste and a tube of inexpensive hand-cream. No make-up, no hairbrush, none of the thousand-and-one "essential" personal care items and products that cluttered my bathroom back in Decatur. This could be the bathroom adjoining a cheap hotel room.

When I emerged again into the hallway, I became conscious of a musty smell. Pierre had opened the door to a small room – just an under-the-stairs storage space really – across from the bathroom. A shelving unit held cleaning products and toilet tissue. Tucked under the lowest stairs was a front-loading combined washer-dryer machine, the only up-to-date item I had seen so far. A green light twinkled from the controls, indicating that a laundry cycle had finished and the machine awaited unloading. I reached down automatically to open the door, but before I touched it, Pierre spoke.

"Careful. There are mice." As he said the words, there was a scurry of movement along the floor, and I reared backwards into the corridor knocking him sideways. He recovered and grabbed my arm to keep me upright.

"Ugh! I hate the things. So that's what the smell is." Peering gingerly through the open door, I noticed the tell-tale droppings on the floor and the gnawed bottom edge of the toilet tissue package. "Chantal left a load of laundry in the machine. That's strange if she was planning a trip, even a short one."

"Yes. Let's see what's upstairs." I was happy to let Pierre go first again, turning on lights and opening doors as we explored the bedrooms. There were two. In the one on the left at the top of the stairs, the double bed was stripped to the mattress and the closet and drawers were empty except for dust balls. Chantal's somewhat larger room was on the right. Perhaps here I would finally gain some insight into the personality of the woman I had come to France to find.

The bed was neatly made. In a curtained alcove hung dresses, skirts, and a couple of jackets, all simple in style and varying in color from grey to brown to navy blue – no prints or even stripes. I moved over to the chest of drawers. Was I really going to go through Chantal's underwear? I remembered when my house in Decatur had been broken into; the feeling of violation had made me nauseous. Conscious of Pierre watching me, I steeled myself and went rapidly from top to bottom, pulling a drawer out, looking in, feeling underneath neatly-folded garments for anything solid, hard-edged or otherwise out of place. Nothing, just underwear, all white, and sweaters and shirts in the same drab color range as the clothes in the make-shift closet. I walked to the other side of the bed. On a small nightstand lay a French translation of a John Grisham novel on top of what looked like a book of spiritual essays. I picked up a photograph in an attractive silver frame: an upper body shot of a woman about my age and a young girl, perhaps ten years old. It was nicely done, looked recent, probably by a professional photographer. It captured the pair laughing as they inclined their heads towards each other in a natural un-posed way. If this woman was Chantal, who was the child?

"Look at this." Pierre held another framed photograph which he had found on the writing desk under the single dormer window, shuttered tight like all the others. The desk had a delicacy missing from the downstairs furniture, and I guessed it was an antique, perhaps the one beloved piece brought from the Limoges apartment Chantal had shared with her mother for all those years. "This is how I remember her."

I took the photo from him, also a studio portrait, but much more formal, in black and white. A beautiful woman, dark hair swept up into a smooth chignon, seated in a carved wooden chair. At her shoulder stood a younger woman, her hand on the chair-back. Claire Dubenoit and her daughter Chantal. Although I was immediately sure of the identity of the subjects, they demonstrated no obvious family resemblance. Claire wore a white silk shirt, the collar elegantly turned up at the back to emphasize her long neck. Her face was turned a quarter to the side, but her large dark eyes were on the camera and a small Mona Lisa smile played on her lips, hinting at flirtation. In contrast, Chantal's expression was serious, even dour. Her hair was cut in a bob, heavy bangs obscuring her eyebrows, and the sides squaring off a round, almost flat face. Her eyes were heavy-lidded, impossible to read. On closer examination, I saw that the hand on the chair was curled into a fist. Comparing it to the photograph of the woman and child on the nightstand, it was hard to believe they depicted the same woman. It was not the difference of perhaps twenty years between the two shots, but the difference in expression and mood.

There was another framed photograph on the desk, this one a snapshot of an older couple standing in front of the Dubenoit half of Le Bec.

"The grandparents?" As I moved to pick it up, I saw a familiar small black box with a winking red eye hidden behind it: a wifi router. So Chantal was on the internet and probably had an email account! No laptop or tablet on the writing desk or anywhere else we had seen, so I guessed she had taken her device with her. However, the fact that she had a life on the web was good news: it might give a tech expert a way to trace her.

"Perhaps there is some correspondence in the desk?" Pierre suggested. Cheered by the discovery of the router, I attacked the writing desk's drawers with none of my earlier scruples, but, except for paper clips, pens, a few clean envelopes and an empty notepad, there was nothing: no bills, no bank statements, no address book, not even a take-out pizza menu.

"Maybe she managed everything online," I was thinking out loud. "It just seems strange that there's nothing personal at all. Almost as if she – or someone – had gone through and cleared out every trace of her."

"Except the washing machine," Pierre said.

"Yes, and these photographs. Do you think it would be OK if I took them – the ones of Chantal, I mean? They might be helpful when I go to Limoges tomorrow."

"You're asking for my permission? They are not my photographs." Pierre seemed affronted that I had asked. Why *had* I asked? Was it an appeal to the moral authority he carried as a priest? Or was I unconsciously trying to convert him into my accomplice? It certainly would be nice to have an ally in my investigation – one who wasn't five thousand miles away.

Pierre looked down at the portrait of Chantal with her mother. His expression softened.

"If you are worried about her, and you think these can help you find her, then, yes, it makes sense. Let me help you remove them from the frames." Pierre turned over the frame and gently eased back the clasps that kept the backing in place. I performed the same maneuver with the framed photograph from the nightstand. I carefully placed both photographs between the pages of the notebook I had brought with me in my shoulder bag.

We retreated through the house, turning off lights as we went. Pierre locked the door and we stood outside, awkwardly speechless, staring at the ground. It was dusk now, and I was eager to get back to St. Barthélemy and write up my first report for Sam and Dykstra, but I didn't want to leave Le Bec without somehow firming up my acquaintance with Pierre with a promise of a future meeting. He broke the silence, as if in answer to my unspoken thought.

"Look, if you like, I can introduce you to the curé. He doesn't speak English so I could be your interpreter. He spoke to Chantal before she disappeared so perhaps ..... He was good friends with my mother, and me too .... before ..." Pierre was hesitant. Maybe he was embarrassed to be offering help to a strange American woman who had appeared out of nowhere. Before he could withdraw the offer, I jumped in.

"Thank you so much. Yes, that would be wonderful. I'll see what else I can find out in Limoges tomorrow, and then shall I call you?"

"Where are you staying? The Hotel Montbrun? I'll come find you."

We shook hands on it, and, after thanking him again, I managed to drive away down the track without crashing the gears or stalling.

The church square in St. Barthélemy was much livelier now, and it was hard to find a parking space. Old men in ancient suits filled several of the benches, attempting to ignore the screaming children hurtling around them. Self-conscious teenagers hunched over surreptitious cigarettes, while an older generation sat sipping aperitifs at the café tables on the sidewalk. I thought about dinner, but decided my need for sleep trumped my need for food. The little Spar market – European equivalent to a 7-11 -- was still open, so I bought a bottle of water, crackers and grapes, and headed for the hotel.

In the lobby, a young family sat transfixed by a soccer game on a wall-mounted TV I had not noticed before; whether they were hotel guests or friends of the owner I could not guess. A stout middle-aged woman had replaced the proprietor at the registration desk. She confirmed that my room came with "*wee-fee*" and gave me the code.

Once in my room, I hurried to connect up my laptop. I was momentarily disappointed not to see an e-mail from Dykstra in my in-box, but I immediately pushed down the heartache, reminding myself he was multiple time zones away and busy with his book tour. I hurried to reduce my mental notes to writing before exhaustion overtook me. It took almost half an hour to complete the report to Sam and Dykstra. When I read it through, I was dismayed at how little real information it contained. I had narrated my conversation with Pierre and described the search in detail – too much detail? Was I trying to justify myself and prepare the ground for mission failure? Clearly, I needed a good night's sleep before I could see things in better proportion. I summarized my tentative conclusions: Chantal probably left Le Bec near the beginning of April; she evidently planned to return before now; and she left surprisingly little trace of her residence at the farmhouse.

I hit 'send' and closed the computer decisively. The bed beckoned me, but before succumbing, I pulled out the two photographs I had taken from Le Bec. I examined them carefully for a resemblance to Sam. Perhaps in the older Chantal, the smiling one, I could see it: high cheekbones, the lines crinkling the corners of her eyes. I turned to the other photo and noted again the closed fist. Then, intuition struck me like a blow to the chest: she *hated* her mother. In a flash, I was back in the icy-hot grip of childhood: the mix of fear, powerlessness and disgust that had driven me to reject my poor excuse for family when I was in my young teens, and still kept me warily circling the possibility of a long-term relationship with anyone. But Chantal wasn't me; she had stayed. Perhaps I was exaggerating the pang of recognition I felt. The camera may have caught the mood of a moment, but not the reality of her feelings for her mother. I would, I hoped, know more tomorrow.

Chapter 8

France - Tuesday

It was wonderful what a good night's sleep and a leisurely breakfast could do. I woke at seven to the tolling of the hour on the church clock. Lying there in the half-light from the open but shuttered window, I wondered how I managed to sleep all night through the din of the repeated bells. I sleepily concluded they must have been silenced during the night-time hours at the request of the citizenry, otherwise only the deaf could get any rest. As I worked this out, I became conscious of a delicious aroma of coffee wafting up from the terrace below. I threw open the shutters and leant out, to be confronted by half a dozen curious upturned faces. Mumbling *"bonjour,"* I stumbled backwards onto the bed. My brief glance of the terrace had revealed a buffet laden with breads, a bowl of fruit, another filled with hard-boiled eggs, and a plate of thin-sliced ham, as well as several smaller tables, two of which were occupied.

Fifteen minutes later, I made my entrance onto the terrace, singing out a cheerful good morning, as if that bleary-eyed, tousled head poking out of the upstairs window had been someone else entirely, if not a figment of the other guests' imagination. An older couple responded in British-accented French. I assumed they were retired vacationers, perhaps on the hunt for a home in "Dordogneshire" like many of their compatriots before them, attracted by a kinder climate, leisurely lifestyle, and French country cooking. The young family I had seen watching soccer the night before occupied a second table: an attractive dark-haired couple who looked too young to have two equally attractive teenage boys. The four chanted their greeting in unison, smiled politely, then resumed their animated and impossible-to-penetrate conversation laced with idioms and contractions – nothing like the French I had been taught in school.

Madame la patronne arrived with a French press coffee pot and a jug of hot milk. She invited me to serve myself from the buffet, and to call her if I needed anything else. I could not imagine what. This was heaven: sitting on a sunlit terrace, flanked by centuries-old ivy-clad stone walls, the aromas of fresh-baked bread and strong coffee blending around me. For this one moment of perfection, I felt completely right in space and time. Of course, as soon as I recognized the feeling, the usual demons rushed in to undermine it: anticipation of the obstacles ahead, guilt at abandoning my work in Atlanta, and doubt again in my wisdom in undertaking this journey. One day, I was going to take a serious look at Buddhism. I really ought to learn to live in the moment. One day, but not yet.

***

The drive to Limoges took about an hour. I had transcribed directions from Google Maps to the apartment Chantal and her mother had occupied until Claire's death, but they conflicted with the city's one-way system and traffic signs to *"toutes directions."* I circled around in frustration for fifteen minutes. Finally, sensing I was near enough to my destination, I snagged a parking spot on the Boulevard Victor Hugo and started walking.

Limoges is a mid-sized city with an ancient center. The online guide I consulted back in Atlanta, was lukewarm about the place. It hadn't flat-out described it as stuffy and bourgeois, but reading between the lines, I gained the impression that Limoges wasn't a tourist hot-spot – or any other kind of hot-spot for that matter. This concurred with my impression of Chantal's family: the over-bearing dentist grandfather and his pretensions to country squire-dom, the mother who, after her student adventures in Paris, never strayed again, and Chantal herself with her drab wardrobe in monotone colors. The Impressionist artist Auguste Renoir hailed from Limoges, but had escaped to Paris as soon as he scraped together the train fare. The locals probably wouldn't have appreciated his rosy nudes. There was the obligatory Gothic cathedral, remnants of medieval city walls, and the recently-discovered crypt of a minor fifth-century saint, but the architectural style of most of the buildings reflected the solid if uninspiring virtues of the Victorian era.

After one inquiry, I was standing on the sidewalk opposite the building where Chantal had spent most of her life. Like its neighbors, the nineteenth-century town house had been converted, with a shop on the ground floor, and living space on the upper two floors. The shutters on the upstairs apartment were closed, but I knew that did not necessarily mean it was unoccupied. Without air-conditioning, keeping the shutters closed was how residents preserved the night-time cool into the heat of the summer day. However, a small sign affixed to the shutters – "*A louer*" and a phone number – indicated that Chantal's apartment was still vacant.

I crossed the street. The shop window contained an elegantly-set dinner table with a large floral centerpiece that obscured the space beyond. The name above the window gave no clue, but as soon as I entered I understood that this was an emporium for Limoges' most famous product: the kaolin-based porcelain that was decorated, painted, exported and imitated all over the world. Here, though, was the basic form: every plate, dish and bowl, as well as a vast variety of vessels for which I could only guess the use, was translucent milky-white, the only ornamentation a cut-out design or raised frieze. The simple monochrome effect took my breath away.

A tall thin woman, equally monochrome with white hair and a black dress glided towards me from the back, a predatory smile on her lips.

"*C'est la vraie porcelaine de Limoges. Tres belle, n'est-ce pas?*"

I agreed, but knew I had to quickly change the subject before she started the hard sell, and I was trapped into purchasing something I could not afford, much less transport back to the US in one piece. I introduced myself, and asked if she knew Claire and Chantal Dubenoit who used to live in the apartment above.

The woman looked me up and down with narrowed eyes and pursed lips, as if calculating whether it was worth her while to answer me. The calculation must have come out in my favor. After all, it was a slow morning; she had no other customers.

"Certainly, I knew them, but not well. Madame Dubenoit – Claire, I suppose – did not go out much, and her daughter rarely stopped by to speak. You know that Madame Dubenoit died, and her daughter moved away?"

"Yes. I'm trying to locate her. Do you have any idea where she might be, or maybe who might know where she is?"

Another few seconds of calculation.

"No idea where she is, but you could ask the agents for the building. The daughter owns it now after her mother's death. This shop too. I want to buy the place, but the agent says she's not interested in selling. If you find her, perhaps you would be kind enough to tell me. Perhaps if I contact her directly, she may change her mind."

I didn't want to make any promises; there was something vaguely threatening in the tone in which she made that last remark.

"Is the agent's phone number the one on the "for rent" sign on the shutter upstairs? Is there a particular name I should ask for?"

"Wait a minute," she glided to the back of the shop and returned after a minute with a business card.

" '*Paulette Marsac, Agence Immobilière d'Ouest, rue Gay Lussac 45, Limoges,*' " I read aloud. "Is that close by?"

"About ten minutes." The elegant *vendeuse* gave me directions, and I set off. As I walked, I rehearsed my approach to Paulette Marsac, wondering whether she was old or young, whether her English might be better than my French, and most of all whether the message she had passed on that the owner "wasn't interested" in selling the building indicated that she was currently in touch with Chantal.

The front window of the agency was filled with photographs of "charming" *fermettes*, "tranquil" villas and stone barns "with great potential." I pushed open the door and entered a small office with two desks facing each other. Neither was occupied. As the door clacked shut behind me, a young man with blond hair and skinny jeans emerged from a door at the back. He came forward with the same salesperson's smile I had met at the porcelain shop. I made a quick decision not to immediately disclose my mission: a gut reaction of distrust that I couldn't explain.

"May I speak to Paulette Marsac, please."

"I'm afraid she's not here. May I help you?"

"When will she be back?"

His manner became a little frosty.

"I really couldn't say. What is it regarding?"

"I'm interested in the property at rue Montaigne, the apartment for rent."

"Yes, that is Paulette's listing," he replied reluctantly. "But I can show it to you. Let me get the details." He went over to a file cabinet and pulled out several fliers. Then, indicating that I should sit, he took the chair across the desk, and assumed his sales patter.

"You are looking for an apartment of character close to the center? We have several very attractive properties. Here is the one you mentioned," placing a flier in front of me on the desk, then immediately covering it with another. "And this is a little closer to the old town, with a view of the river, same square meters. Or you might like to look at a more modern building—"

"Thank you, but I think I'd like to start with rue Montaigne. Can you reach Madame Marsac?"

The young man pouted, all pretense of charm abandoned. He got up and flounced towards the back of the office, speaking rapidly into his cell phone.

"She's on her way," he threw the remark over his shoulder as he disappeared into the back room from which he had originally emerged.

I examined the description of Chantal's old apartment carefully. The photographs showed plain, high-ceilinged rooms, empty of furniture, with wide-planked oak floors. The kitchen and bathroom were old-fashioned, and probably had not been updated for fifty years. Where was the furniture now? Not at the farmhouse, except perhaps the little antique *ecritoire* in Chantal's bedroom. I pondered the flier, and what this information added, if anything, to my picture of Chantal.

It was close to noon, less than half an hour after I had entered the *agence*, when the door opened and a burst of color came through. Paulette was a large woman with hair tinted the improbable magenta that French women favor. Her mango-hued top strained across her substantial cleavage, a floral-print skirt swirled around her ample hips. She whipped off her sunglasses with one hand and extended the other.

"I'm so sorry you had to wait. I was taking measurements." She had a smoker's voice, throaty and deep, and a smile that wrinkled her eyes. I guessed she was forty but I could have been ten years off in either direction. The sulky young man came out of the back room, looking pale and insignificant in comparison to Paulette's bright bulk.

"I'm going to lunch now. You lock up, OK?" and without a glance at me, he squeezed past Paulette and left through the street door.

"So, you are interested in renting the apartment on rue Montaigne? Shall we go and take a look?" Before I could say anything, she snatched up a bunch of keys from the desk, and ushered me out to the street. She flicked over the "*Ouvert*" sign to "*Fermé*," locked the door behind her and started off down the sidewalk. I didn't move, forcing her to turn and come back to me.

"Well, yes, I'd like to see the apartment, but I must be honest. I'm not in the market to rent it. I'm looking for Chantal Dubenoit. I'm a friend of her father's. He has been unable to reach her. I went to the place near St Barthélemy where she was living, and she's disappeared. I was hoping you might know where Chantal is or have some way to trace her." I was holding my breath. Paulette was now my best lead, but even if she could help me, *would* she?

Paulette's slightly protuberant eyes blinked several times before she spoke.

"Hmm. Chantal is not at Le Bec?" I shook my head. Paulette spoke thoughtfully, "I haven't spoken to her for months, and she doesn't respond to e-mails."

"You have her e-mail address? Her cell phone number?" I couldn't keep the excitement out of my voice. These were the clues that might allow Dykstra's investigator to trace her.

"Ye-es, but if she doesn't respond...? Look, it's lunchtime. Why don't we get something to eat and talk about this?" Without waiting for a response, Paulette was off again. For a large woman she moved fast with small steps that left her breathless. We didn't speak again until she plonked herself down at a sidewalk table outside an unprepossessing bistro called Chez Gaby.

"I recommend the *plat du jour*."

"OK. What is it?"

Paulette gave a raspy laugh. "I don't know! But it's always good." She waved at someone in the interior of the restaurant and raised two fingers. Clearly, she was well-known here. Within minutes, a waiter brought a basket of bread and a demi-carafe of red wine, stopping to exchange some unintelligible quip that had Paulette roaring with laughter.

While we waited for our meal, Paulette grilled me pleasantly, but relentlessly, discovering my age, occupation, marital status, as well as my relationship to Sam, and the reason I had volunteered to come to France in search of his estranged daughter. We were soon speaking an ungainly mix of French and English. Her English was rapid-fire and colloquial, but totally ignored the rules of grammar. She substituted French words, rather than search for the right one in English. I plodded on in my schoolgirl French for a while, but when it started to take too long to translate my thoughts into speech, I abandoned the struggle and started to speak English too.

After we dug into the *poulet basquaise* – a delicious chicken stew with tomatoes, red peppers and spicy sausage – we got back to Chantal's disappearance.

"The woman at the porcelain shop said you told her Chantal doesn't want to sell. When did Chantal tell you that?"

"*Vraiment*, Chantal didn't say that. After her mother's death, we discussed selling. She said she goes to think about it. But when I make the e-mail to Chantal to say I have an offer to buy, no response. The *porcelainière* always asks, and *finalement*, I tell her Chantal is not interested. It is good for me if she sells: big money. But Chantal must say yes. *Alors*, I want to find her also."

"Can you give me her e-mail address and phone number? We may be able to trace her through them."

As Paulette was searching for the information on her smart phone, I remembered the photographs I had taken from the farmhouse.

"Can you confirm that this is Chantal? I'm pretty sure this is her with her mother, but I don't know who the young girl is in the other photo. Do you?"

Paulette froze. Her bronzed face suddenly seemed pinched and sallow.

"*Ou as-tu trouvé ça?*"

"In the farmhouse; in Chantal's bedroom. Why? Who is the little girl?"

"It's my daughter!" Paulette's voice was an ugly rasp. She stared at the photograph, then turned it over. I saw what I had not noticed before: the photography studio's name stamped on the back.

"You didn't know this had been taken?"

"No! I can't imagine.... Oh! I remember! After Madame Dubenoit's death, *novembre, peut-être*. Chantal comes to the *agence*. Francine was there, Saturday, I think, and I must leave with another client. Chantal said she stay with Francine, eat ice-cream. Never she say— this!"

Paulette held the picture out towards me with the tips of her fingers, as if it was burning hot. I took it from her.

"Do you know the studio where this was taken?"

"*Bien sûr*. It's just in this street." Paulette stood up abruptly, and I thought she was going to rush out of the restaurant and down the street to confront the photographer about the picture he had taken six months before. Perhaps, realizing the futility of that gesture, she sank down again into her seat and began tapping feverishly on her phone.

"*Allo?*" There followed a stream of rapid French from which I gathered that Paulette was calling her daughter's school and seeking confirmation that Francine was in class. Once satisfied that she was safe and sound, Paulette put down the phone and hunted in her bag for a cigarette which she lit with a shaking hand. She took a deep drag and exhaled a long stream of smoke. I pushed away my half-finished meal; neither of us was likely to eat another mouthful.

"Can you make sense of this?" I pointed at the photograph; the two faces grinning up from the tablecloth seemed to mock us. Paulette nodded slowly, still inhaling her cigarette as if it was oxygen.

"That day, I come back to the *agence*, Chantal says many nice things about Francine, asks about her *papa*." Paulette made a movement with her mouth that indicated her low opinion of Francine's father. "I tell her he's *un salaud*, a pig. He leave us with nothing!" She leaned over the table to emphasize her next point. "Then she say, 'he leave you good *gènes*; your daughter is beautiful. Perhaps I will find *un papa* with good *gènes* for *mon bébé.*' You see! She wants a baby! She pretends with my Francine; makes a photograph of '*maman et fille,*' but *à la fin* she wants a baby for herself! She is crazy, that one!"

"You think she's gone off to, what? Get pregnant? Adopt a child?" It did make a kind of sense. Finally free of her mother and the cloistered life she had led with her, Chantal was embarking on the second half of her life, biological clock ticking furiously, afraid of growing old alone. A sudden shiver of fear clutched at my chest: how vulnerable she would be to every charlatan and schemer. Having an internet account did not mean she was prepared for all the snares of modern life. She was a forty-year-old innocent out there amongst the wolves, and she had been out there alone for nearly three months now.

Now that Paulette had overcome her immediate panic at the sight of the photo, she was my eager ally in brainstorming theories about Chantal's disappearance and identifying alleys for investigation. The rent from the porcelain shop on rue Montaigne was paid to the agency. After the deduction of the management fee, maintenance and other expenses, the remainder was deposited in Chantal's account at *Banque Paribas.* Good luck there in getting any information about the accountholder's whereabouts -- I knew French law was even more stringent than US law with regard to personal data privacy – but perhaps Dykstra's contact could use the information.

Paulette was puzzled about the furniture from the apartment. She was convinced Chantal had taken it to Le Bec, but my description of the furnishings there did not match. Chantal's car was another mystery: she owned a blue VW Polo, Paulette was certain. Claire had bought it years before and it was rarely driven, just left parked in front of the apartment. It had definitely left with Chantal. Where was it now?

I carefully noted down Chantal's e-mail address and cell phone number. Paulette racked her brains to come up with more details about the Dubenoits, but mother and daughter had been equally reticent about sharing anything personal. Paulette could not remember a single reference to extended family or friends, to favorite places or pastimes. By the time we parted company – Paulette helped me find my way back to my rental car – we were old friends. We exchanged the customary three kisses on alternate cheeks without bumping heads, and promised each other to keep in touch.

I began the forty kilometer drive back to St. Barthélemy in an upbeat mood, anticipating my e-mail report to Sam and Dykstra. Now I had some hard leads.

Chapter 9

France - Tuesday

As I drove back down the RN 21 towards St. Barthélemy, the sun disappeared behind a sheen of high white cloud. Some cumulus was assembling ahead on the southern horizon, presaging a late-day thunder storm. I decided to try and squeeze in a run in advance of the rain. It would give me a chance to organize my thoughts and sort out next steps before e-mailing Sam and Dykstra.

I claimed what I now thought of as "my" parking spot on the square in front of the church. It was siesta time, nothing stirred as I hurried to the hotel, hoping to catch *Monsieur le patron* on duty in the lobby, and get some advice on running routes before he too took an afternoon nap.

"The path along the river, maybe three kilometers to the bridge at Champet. Then you can come back along the path, or, if you want to make a circuit, cross the bridge and return by the road. Not much traffic at this time of day."

Thanking him, I headed up to my room to change.

Of course, I had reached the furthest point of the run when the skies opened. I was quickly drenched. And then, fifteen minutes later, as I squelched back into the square, ringing out the tails of my tee-shirt, the rain stopped as suddenly as it had begun and brilliant sunshine mocked me. I had a twenty-euro bill secreted in the allegedly-waterproof pocket of my running shorts, so I detoured to the Spar to pick up another bottle of water and some crackers to snack on.

I was making my way forward to the single cash register at the front of the little store, awkwardly holding my purchases away from my dripping body, when I saw Pierre. He was leaning against the counter and engaged in friendly conversation with the sales clerk. Again, he looked decidedly un-clerical in faded blue jeans and a white polo shirt. Too late to duck behind the shelves: he had spotted me, and grinned a welcome.

"*Bonjour*! So, how did it go in Limoges?" I was painfully conscious of the wet tee-shirt molded to the sports bra underneath, but he seemed cheerfully oblivious.

"Um, good, I think. I found out some stuff ...." I put the Evian and a box of crackers on the counter, smiling weakly at the teenage sales girl. She looked from me to Pierre, then back again, her mouth hanging slightly open, her eyes wide. I guessed there was not much entertainment in a small town like St. B, and our meeting was livening up her day. She showed no interest in the money I held out in the hope that I could make a quick escape without further embarrassment.

"I was on my way to the hotel to see you. I wondered if you had plans for dinner." Abruptly switching into French, Pierre addressed the girl. "Is Jean-Paul cooking tonight?"

She gulped and blinked before responding. "*Eh, bien sûr.*"

He turned back to me, and spoke again in English, "You can tell me then what you learned in Limoges. Shall I see you in the hotel lobby at eight?"

"Well, erm, yes, that would be …" I was having difficulty stringing words together, even in my native tongue, certain that if I looked down, I would see a puddle around my feet, like I peed myself.

"*Voilà.*" At last, the sales girl rescued me, handing me my change and purchases in a plastic bag.

"*A toute suite,* then." I felt his eyes on my back as I made my way out of the store.

***

It took a long shower (and more banged elbows) before I regained my composure, and could examine thoughtfully why I had become so flustered by my encounter with the priest. Back in Atlanta, I wasn't self-conscious about being seen sweating in my running gear. On the contrary, I felt a sense of superiority that my forty-year-old body was still up for it. I admit, I like – need? – to be in control of every situation. I pride myself on my cool professionalism, of presenting a competent, unflappable demeanor to the world. But since arriving in France, I'd let my guard slip. I was on holiday from the strict norms that governed my everyday existence. I knew no one here, and no one knew me. I had no image to project, no reputation to keep safe. So why did it matter so much that Pierre had seen me semi-clad, rain dripping off my nose, and hair plastered to my forehead? Because I was attracted to him, that's why. Who wouldn't be? He was drop-dead gorgeous. But this was dangerous ground. Less than a year ago, my attraction to Dykstra had proved to be near-fatal. I wasn't about to slide down that slippery slope again, especially with a man of the cloth. I resolutely wrote off my feelings to embarrassment at being caught dripping, and reminded myself I had a task to perform: reporting on my day in Limoges.

The storm had done little to dissipate the late afternoon heat, which, in spite of closing the louvered shutters against the sun before I left for Limoges, had thoroughly penetrated my room. Dressed in just bra and panties, I settled my back against the carved headboard and logged on to my laptop. I read Sam's brief, supportive e-mail, confirming his flight plan out of New York the following Saturday. He would meet up with Dykstra at Heathrow Airport on Sunday morning and continue on to Bordeaux with him. They would rent a car and be in St. Barthélemy by mid-afternoon. I was again disappointed not to see an e-mail from Dykstra, but chided myself that he was probably up to his ears in book tour business.

Ⅰ began my report by laying out what I had learned from Paulette: Chantal's cell phone number and e-mail address, the make and color of her car, and the name of her bank. I didn't understand how Dykstra's contact was going to make use of these details to locate her. I suspected that some shady internet maneuvers would be involved. Best not to inquire into their legality; I just hoped they proved successful. Then I related Paulette's idea about Chantal's eagerness to become a mother. I was beginning to have cold feet about this. The idea had seemed valid in the first flush of identifying Paulette's daughter in what I now thought of as "the happy photo," but it conflicted with the theory I was developing independently: Chantal's strained relationship with her mother. If what I had intuited from the other photo I had found in Chantal's bedroom was real, how could those hostile feelings provide a model on which she might base her own future? Of course, my own experience informed my thoughts on this. I pushed the computer off my knees and stretched out to contemplate the past, an activity I usually avoided, but which had been nudging me just below the level of consciousness ever since Sam first drew the parallels between my life and Chantal's.

One word to describe my mother: ineffectual. She even looked washed-out: pale grey eyes, stringy fair hair, emaciated to the point of transparency. She had been a beauty once, she told me. She ran away to London in the Swinging Sixties at fifteen years old, and immersed herself in the exploding music scene. She was Twiggy-thin, Biba eyes peering out from under Jane Asher bangs, a tailor-made groupie whose claim to fame consisted of her presence at the 1969 party where the Rolling Stones' Brian Jones drowned in his own swimming pool. But by then, she'd already had a child, my half-brother Shane, and was, more often than not, addled by drugs. Perhaps that's what drew her to my father, himself no stranger to substance abuse. He arrived on the scene, an American draft-dodger with delusions of rock grandeur and a penchant for violence. In my more sentimental moments, I thought she might be as much his victim as I was, but I quickly rejected that picture: *I* was the child; *she* was the adult. It was *her* duty to protect me from him.

With that back story, it was hardly surprising that I never wanted to have a child of my own. I could act appropriately when law school friends with babies pressed me to "just hold him!" but I never felt the tug on the heartstrings that was supposed to result. I got on better with older children, although always glad to hand them back at the end of a boisterous afternoon of play. At forty, I still had the time, but not the inclination, to complicate my life by getting pregnant. I didn't need to read the studies to know that the children of abusive or neglectful parents tend to make poor parents themselves.

In the end, I stated Paulette's theory without adding any comment, signed off and pressed "send."

***

The home-printed packet of local information for guests provided in my room listed two restaurants in St. Barthélemy: one a pizzeria, and the other serving *"menus typique de la région."* The place Pierre led me to was neither of these. We entered through what appeared to be a working men's bar – bright fluorescent lights and scarred formica-topped tables. The customers, all male, muttered the obligatory *"m'sieurs-dames,"* as we passed through to the back.

We descended a narrow curving staircase to another world. Here, the cellar walls were stripped back to their ancient warm brick, the ceiling beams low and blackened by centuries of cooking fires, possibly from the same stone oven that occupied the far corner – thankfully unlit on this warm June night. Sparkling white linen clothed five tables, of which four were already occupied. The other guests ranged in age and ethnicity, but all looked well-heeled and casually elegant. An air of excited anticipation suffused the room.

The change in ambience from the upstairs bar was disorienting, and I stood still to absorb it, as well as the seductive aroma of garlic and roasting meat, while Pierre rushed forward to greet a young man who I assumed was Jean Paul, our host and chef. They embraced warmly, and I flashed the thought that perhaps Pierre might be gay before reminding myself that French men weren't so squeamish about demonstrating physical affection as Americans or Brits. Pierre quickly introduced me before Jean Paul disappeared into the kitchen. Apparently, he had been waiting for us to arrive before starting to plate the first course.

Pierre explained that Jean Paul spent nine months of the year as *sous-chef* at one of the most prestigious restaurants in Montreal. This was his second summer trying to build a reputation for himself in France, hoping to attract a rich foodie who would sponsor him in his own restaurant. His father owned the bar; his mother and sister – the teenage sales clerk from the little market on the square – helped in the kitchen and would serve us.

A hush fell as medallions of seared *foie gras* accompanied by a dollop of fig jam and wafer-thin toasts appeared in front of us. We all waited as Jean Paul's mother poured tiny glasses of straw-colored wine, and then we reverently lifted forks to mouths. Three seconds later, a collective "aah" provoked grins and chuckles all round, before the buzz of conversation resumed. I began to understand how privileged I was to participate in this feast. The other diners had probably booked weeks in advance, and were now having to squeeze their elbows in to accommodate an additional table laid at the last minute for us. I was glad at least that I had made an extra effort to erase the drowned rat image of my afternoon encounter with Pierre. I wore the cream linen shift that had last seen the light of day at the Marriott Bar in New York, with my hair in a loosely-structured up-do, and dangly earrings.

After we had paid appropriate attention to the food, I described my day in Limoges.

"So, did she answer?"

I looked at Pierre in bemusement, failing to understand his question. He continued, "Perhaps she has turned off the phone or the battery is dead. Better to e-mail."

Heat rushed to my cheeks. I felt like a complete idiot. It had never occurred to me to try the cell phone number Paulette had given me, or the e-mail address. I had just passed them on to Sam and Dykstra like a good little automaton, obeying orders, leaving it to the big boys to join the dots.

"I'll call her tonight, *and* send an e-mail. Of course! I should have thought of that!" Even if Chantal had not responded to Paulette's messages, she might answer mine. After all, I had a compelling story to tell her: *your father is searching for you. He is coming to France and wants very much to see you.*

"Do you still want to meet the curé? I can take you tomorrow morning, if you like."

"Oh, yes. I think I should pursue all leads. It may take a while before I hear back from her, if I ever do. Anyway, I want to understand as much as I can about her before Sam arrives. Tomorrow would be great, if you can spare the time...." I couldn't work out exactly why he wanted to help me, but I was glad he did.

"Sure, it's no problem."

Emboldened by the wine, and the relaxed feeling of well-being that comes with good food – we had now progressed through a chilled mango gazpacho served in a martini glass to the *plat principal,* slow-roasted lamb with an orange and redcurrant sauce, and crispy garlic-rosemary potatoes – I leaned forward, smiling, my chin on my hands.

"So, what kind of priest are you? I mean, you don't wear priest clothes, or do, er, priest things, like ...." Oops, I had gone too far. I could sense Pierre closing up, retreating from me, even though he had not moved. "I'm sorry, that's rude—"

"No, it's fine," but it wasn't. "I'm a priest *en vacances*, I have no duties. Since my mother died, my order has given me ...." For once, he was at a loss for the English word, "... a sabbatical." I waited for him to say more, but he didn't. I suppressed my curiosity and concentrated my attention on my plate. The chatter of the other diners swirled around us, disguising the awkwardness of our silence. I needed to bridge the gap that had opened between us, and steer the conversation back to neutral territory.

"I still don't understand what happened to the furniture, Chantal's furniture from the Limoges apartment. Paulette is convinced it came with her to Le Bec, but it's not in the house, is it? Unless—"

Pierre smacked his forehead. "But of course! The barn!"

I thought of the wooden building next to the farmhouse. The doors had stood wide open yesterday, and I had seen no sign of furniture. Seeing my puzzled frown, Pierre explained.

"The old stone barn on the lane as you approach. It has no electricity so the farmer who rents the land and the other farm buildings does not want it. *Maman* stored old stuff there, our bicycles, some tools. I bet she let Chantal put her furniture there. It's huge, plenty of room."

"Can we take a look tomorrow, after talking to the curé?"

"Certainly."

The meal wound down. After dessert – wild strawberries sprinkled with kirsch on an almond crust – Jean Paul emerged from the kitchen to accept the praise of his satisfied customers. As they drained their glasses and fumbled for their wallets, he pulled up a chair to our table. I wondered where our bill was, and how I could manage to gracefully pay at least my share.

"You enjoyed it?"

"It was sublime!"

Content to sit back, I listened to Pierre and Jean Paul exchange rapid-fire colloquial French. They had grown up together and had their own jargon that was impenetrable to me, especially after several glasses of wine and the *vieux marc* that Jean Paul produced after the last of the other guests had exited. The men's laughter and obvious pleasure in each other's company was infectious, but the alcohol and remnants of jetlag were taking their toll: I could feel my eyelids drooping.

"That was the best meal of my life, but I must be getting back. No, Pierre, you stay here and catch up." But he insisted on accompanying me, which turned out to be a good thing. It was close to midnight when we emerged into the night air, and the contrast with the overheated cellar made me dizzy. I was grateful for Pierre's hand under my elbow, guiding me through the narrow streets back to the Hotel Montbrun. When I fumbled with the key that would let me into the hotel after hours, he took it from me and opened the door. For one brief moment, I thought he was going to kiss me, but before I could sort out my reaction to that thought, he stepped back and extended his hand for a formal shake.

"I'll come tomorrow at nine, O.K.?"

"Yes. Goodnight. Oh, what do I do about paying for the meal? Will you get the money to Jean Paul?"

Pierre smiled.

"There is no charge. Believe me, the other *gourmets* at dinner tonight have covered the costs. Maybe you can tell your rich friends about his cooking when you get back to America, and they will invest in his restaurant?"

I laughed.

"I don't think I have any rich friends, but I'll do my best. Goodnight."

"Goodnight. *A demain.*"

Chapter 10

France - Wednesday

Without noticing, I had passed the entrance to the curé's residence several times on the brief walk between the square where I parked the rental car and the hotel: a plain wooden door set in a high stone wall. Pierre opened the door and preceded me into a small paved courtyard huddled in the shadow of the south wall of the parish church. He seemed nervous this morning, and I wondered if he was uncomfortable about his offer to introduce me to the parish priest and act as interpreter for our meeting. Or perhaps dinner last night had pushed our relationship to a level he now regretted, and he wanted to back away. I resolved to be friendly but business-like going forward. I didn't want to jeopardize his reputation in the town – or his help in my quest.

Pierre rapped on the door to the presbytery. I hung back to leave him the space to explain the purpose of our visit before introducing me, but he was not given the chance. The priest who opened the door was almost as wide as he was tall. He had a round pink face and a monkish fringe of white hair circling a bald pate. His black suit was shiny with age, and the Roman collar less than bright-white. He started in on Pierre without any preliminary greeting, gesturing with both hands to heaven. I had no problem understanding his emphatic language.

"Finally, you come! It's more than a month since your mother's funeral. Nearly two months! You cannot turn your back like this! We must talk!" The curé started dragging Pierre inside, drowning out the younger man's attempts to speak. Finally, Pierre freed an arm and pointed back at me.

"Father Joseph! Please! This lady needs your help to find Chantal Dubenoit. We will talk about, er ... my situation later, but I told her that you knew Chantal and might have an idea where she is."

Father Joseph looked me up and down, scowling ferociously. Then, as suddenly as he had attacked Pierre, his face cleared, and, beaming, he stood aside to wave me into his residence.

"Chantal Dubenoit, eh? She's still missing? I was sure she'd return by now." The volatile little priest bustled ahead into what I guessed was his study: a scarred desk under the one small window, bookshelves covering one wall, and a tattered sofa pushed against another.

"Sit! Sit!" He indicated the sofa and we obediently sat down. "Coffee? Tea? No?" He gave us no time to answer before rushing on. "I was surprised she did not come to the funeral. Your *maman* was a good friend to her, but then they had not known each other long, and some young people cannot support funerals."

I didn't comment that Chantal was over forty, so could hardly count as young.

He continued, "How do you know Mademoiselle Dubenoit? Are you a friend from Limoges?"

I cleared my throat, and spoke carefully, hoping he would give me time to explain myself in my halting French.

"I do not know Chantal. I am a friend of her father's. He has not seen her for many years, but he wants to...." I searched in vain for the French equivalent of "reconnect," before settling on, "He wants to help her now that her mother is dead. He has tried to contact her, and he came here in April to see her, but she had already disappeared."

"American?" The old man's brows plunged low over his piercing blue eyes.

I nodded tentatively, hoping this wasn't a black mark against me.

"And her father is American too?"

I nodded again.

Father Joseph puffed out his lips. He looked at Pierre.

"Why do you think I know anything about this?" His voice sounded challenging, but I was rapidly gaining the impression that this was just his demeanor: a cross between a pit bull terrier and one of the Seven Dwarfs in priestly garb – probably Grumpy.

"Because my mother told me in a letter before she died that she asked you to speak to Chantal. Chantal was troubled, and *maman* was sure you could help her."

We waited to see if this appeal to the priest's vanity would be effective. He sniffed, and, still directing himself to Pierre, spoke in a reproving tone.

"You above all should know that I cannot reveal the confidences of the confessional."

Pierre's voice was placating. "But if it was not a confession, and if she is hurt or in danger, and if you can help reunite her with her only remaining family ….."

Father Joseph considered, his head tilted to one side, bird-like.

"*Eh, bien,* I don't know where she is, but it is true that she was troubled. No, *not* troubled: excited, obsessed perhaps, rather than troubled. I thought even a little deranged. It is necessary to understand that her life until she came to Le Bec was very protected, very quiet. Her mother controlled everything. Then, suddenly, the mother dies and Mademoiselle Chantal has money, freedom! But she has no training, no career, no purpose! *Alors*, she searches for a *projet*, a cause, and she decides: the children! She will help the children! Children who have been maltreated and abused. I try to explain to her that for this work she needs training, but she is so impatient! I give her the address of the Catholic Children's Services in Limoges, where perhaps she can observe, but she says, no, she has found an opportunity on the Internet. There, she can work directly with the children."

I forced myself to speak calmly.

"Do you know where this opportunity is? Who it is with?"

He shrugged.

"No. She refused to say, except that it is a safe place, *la bastide*, where the children can be kept protected from their parents."

"Is there anything, anything at all, that Chantal said that might reveal where she went?"

He shook his head. "I will telephone the CCS in Limoges to find out if this 'safe place' is known to them. That is all I can think to do."

That was something, at least. And I could do an Internet search to try to follow Chantal's steps across the worldwide web. On the whole, things looked promising. Piece by piece, I was gaining a picture of who she was and what motivated her. If she responded to the e-mail I had sent earlier this morning, the puzzle of her disappearance might be complete before Sam and Dykstra arrived.

Because of the late hour, and, yes, the amount of wine I had consumed, I had postponed calling Chantal on her cell phone when I got back to the hotel the night before. When I tried the number before breakfast, I listened to an unfamiliar tone repeating for more than two minutes, far longer than the usual time to roll over to voice-mail. The cell phone account was now apparently out of action for some unknown reason. So instead, I wrote a carefully phrased e-mail, explaining my relationship to her father, letting her know that he would shortly be in France, and that he was very much looking forward to seeing her. I gave her several ways to contact me, and offered to meet her wherever and whenever she liked. I closed, hoping she was well, and promising to provide any additional information she needed. After sending the message, I remained logged on for several minutes in case I received an "undeliverable" notice. I didn't, so, as long as she was checking her in-box, she would read it. Whether she would respond was another question.

Pierre stood up, no doubt eager to make his escape before Father Joseph launched into another tirade. I followed suit.

"Thank you so much. This has been very helpful."

The curé brushed past me, ignoring my outstretched hand, and making a grab for Pierre's arm.

"We must talk! The monsignor has written--- "

"I can't stay. I have to ..." Pierre was attempting to use me as a human shield as he scuttled backwards towards the door. "Tomorrow!"

We made an ungainly exit through the courtyard. Once we were on the street outside, I turned to Pierre.

"What on earth was that all about?"

He laughed, a bit ashamed, I thought.

"Oh, Father Joseph has known me since I was a baby. He thinks I'm still a baby! I haven't been to see him as often as he'd like, that's all."

I let it go, although I felt there was more to it. I had been too intrusive the night before, and as a result felt the chill of his withdrawal. I didn't want to risk that again.

"O.K. I followed most of what he said but I don't know this word '*bastide*.' What does it mean?"

"A '*bastide*' is the French word for fortress. You know, the center part of a medieval castle."

"The keep? I see. I thought it was the name of the children's home Chantal told him about. Could that be possible?"

Pierre shrugged again.

"I don't know. I don't remember any places with that name when I was growing up here. But there are several '*bastides*' – ruined castles – around here. You know that Richard *Coeur de Lion* – Richard the Lionheart – died in the castle at Châlus; it's about twenty kilometers from here."

"Hmm." I vaguely remembered covering the period during my spotty English primary school education, but all that stuck about King Richard was his evil brother Prince John who tried to usurp the throne during Richard's absence in France. Not helpful to my present quest. "Shall we explore that barn?"

***

The barn's huge double doors that faced onto the lane were padlocked, and Pierre had no idea where the key was. He said he remembered a small, human-sized entrance on the opposite end which he was confident would be unlocked, so we pushed our way through the nettles and other undergrowth that grew at waist-height along the side of the ancient stone building.

"We should have stopped at the house for a flashlight," he said, straining to open the small door at the back. Years of disuse had stiffened the hinges. While he struggled, I stepped back to look around. The barn was about sixty feet long and half as wide. The walls reared up twenty feet, windowless except for some unglazed slits near the roof, probably more for airflow than to provide daylight to the interior. I could see the smooth egg-like protuberances of swallows' nests tucked into the shadow of the eaves. The building would also be a haven for bats as well as other small creatures. I shuddered involuntarily. I'm not a huge fan of flora and fauna, at least, not the fauna part, and especially not the rodent variety.

The door opened part-way but refused to budge further. Pierre peered in.

"I'll go first. Be careful! It's a mess in here."

I followed, stopping just inside to let my eyes adjust to the gloom. Gradually, tall shapes resolved themselves into armoires and stacks of cardboard boxes. These had been lined up closest to the back of the barn, and were the reason the door we had come through was partially blocked. The air smelt stale, with an odor that immediately brought to mind the closet under the stairs at Chantal's place with its mice droppings and abandoned laundry. A layer of dust prickled my nose. I edged my way around the side of the makeshift barrier to be confronted with a forest of chair legs and small tables stacked on top of larger tables. These may have been arranged in an orderly fashion once, but in the half-light they resembled a haphazard furniture jungle.

"Do you think this is Chantal's stuff?" I called to Pierre who had already reached the space in front of the double doors. I blundered around, hitting my shins against unseen objects, as I tried to find a passage through to him. The smell was stronger here.

"Here's her car!" He shouted. "Blue VW, right?"

"That's fantastic!" I crashed through a gap and bumped right into Pierre, who was bending down to look through the car window.

"Sarah! Go back! Don't—"

His voice sounded choked, and should have warned me, but it was too late. I was already next to him, leaning forward to peer through the passenger-side window. Seated in the driver's seat, the head turned towards us, was a body. In the near-darkness, its face glowed white and skull-like, dark empty holes for eyes, the mouth pulled open into a tight O of surprise. The hair showed it was a woman, or had been once: thick, long and lustrous, like a stage wig placed on a decaying mannequin. The rest of the body was covered in dark clothing. Except for the hand. The right arm extended across the passenger seat, the palm protruding from the sleeve turned up as if offering us something, or inviting us in. There was a dark patch in the center. I thought for the briefest moment that perhaps blood had pooled there, blackening the skin. Then the patch moved, detached itself from the hand and scuttled up the arm to disappear into a narrow gap between clothes and neck. Everything seemed to slow down, and I could hear my blood drumming in my ears. I tried to scream but my throat closed up. Staggering backwards, I fought like a mad thing towards the slim slice of daylight at the back of the barn, hacking at chairs and tables as if they were live antagonists. I could hear Pierre behind me, calling "Sarah! Sarah!" but I couldn't wait for him. With the dreadful slow motion of a nightmare, I approached the door, my breath now coming in ragged gasps. I finally made my way through to the light, stumbled a few feet, then retched repeatedly into the weeds.

"Is that her? Is that Chantal?" Hands on knees, I craned up at Pierre who stood with his hand on my bent back. He formed a black outline against the brightness of the sun. I couldn't see his expression, but I could hear the grimness in his voice.

"I don't know, Sarah, but whoever it is has been dead for a long time. Months, maybe."

Chapter 11

France - Wednesday

Waiting for the detectives to come and interview me, I sat again at the table under the arbor on Pierre's terrace, watching the sunlight filter through the vine and sipping a glass of Evian. Had it really been only two days since I was here before? Just two days since I arrived in France?

Years ago, I read a dumbed-down version of Einstein's theory of relativity that discussed the elasticity of time. I had long forgotten the details, but the afternoon reminded me of the concept, providing another textbook example of time playing tricks. My watch told me only three hours had passed since the discovery of the body, but it seemed to take Pierre and me an age to stumble back up the lane to Le Bec to call the police, and another age until they arrived: two young *gendarmes* wearing freshly-pressed uniforms and supercilious faces as if they thought this was a prank call. When they returned from the barn, their patronizing expressions were gone, replaced by a delicate tinge of green. They huddled over their phones to contact a higher authority. And, again, Pierre and I waited, side by side at his kitchen table, mostly silent, staring down at the much-scrubbed wood. For my part, I was not seeing the table, but instead, on a slow repeating loop, the mouse running up the corpse's arm from skeletal hand to ruined face.

Pierre seemed most distressed that the body had been there so long, perhaps since before his mother had died and before he had returned to live in the farmhouse.

"I should have looked in the barn. I passed it every day. I should have checked!"

"What could you have done if she was already dead?" I said flatly. I was preoccupied with the knowledge that I would have to call Sam and tell him about our discovery. What would I say?

"I could at least have prevented the ….. decay to the body. And I could have given your friend Sam some certainty, avoided his worry over her disappearance."

And I would never have come here, I thought.

"Don't you think Sam would rather have the uncertainty of her disappearance, than the certainty of her death – *if* it's Chantal there in the barn?" But who else could it be?

We lapsed into silence. I felt too drained to try to assuage Pierre's guilt. To be honest, I didn't feel much sympathy for his anguish. It seemed self-centered somehow, like Lady Macbeth's '*What, in our house?*' when the king's murdered body is found. Or perhaps it was a priest thing: the need to take onto his shoulders all the bad things that happen around him. Either way, I couldn't help feeling irritated. I checked myself; I really did not know this man at all.

The *gendarmes* had taken a basic statement from us – mostly from Pierre, as the shock of finding the body had left me numb and tongue-tied, at least in French. They handed this statement on to the next arrivals on the scene: a couple of detectives in civilian clothes, who were in turn followed by a large white van which disgorged a team dressed in haz-mat suits – crime scene technicians, I assumed. Later, an older gentleman – doctor or medical examiner? – drew up in a black BMW. The parking area in front of Le Bec became quite congested. At this point, the detectives summoned Pierre, and told me, politely but firmly, to wait out back on the terrace.

Another hour passed. I sipped my water, and listened to occasional sounds of activity. I looked up once at a noise from Chantal's side of the farmhouse, and saw Pierre opening shutters on the second floor, to let in more light for a search probably. He smiled glumly at me before retreating back into the dimness of the bedroom.

Although I felt exhausted, I knew I had to marshal my thoughts and prepare some questions for the police when they finally got around to interviewing me. First and most importantly, had they been able to identify the body? Second, what was the cause of death? And third, when had she died? I wanted this information before I spoke to Sam.

Suddenly, a wave of homesickness swept over me. I pictured my little Craftsman bungalow, every cornice and door knob as familiar to me as my own body. I wanted to be there so much my chest hurt. And not just the bricks and mortar; the people too: Gerardo, his gruff exterior hiding a fierce loyalty; Heather at the coffee shop, drama queen with a heart of gold. And my new-found friends: 'lasagne Jane,' Perry and his daughters, John and Deb who had offered me a place to stay. My eyes brimmed with tears, and to stave off a full-scale meltdown, I stood up and walked across the grass towards the trees, taking deep breaths, concentrating hard on the inhalation and the exhalation as I had been coached to do when anxiety attacks threatened.

"Mademoiselle McKinney? Can you answer some questions?" The two detectives stood expectantly outside Pierre's back door. I took a moment to settle myself, then turned and walked slowly back to the terrace.

The older of the two did the talking. A large man in a rumpled grey suit, he looked as tired as I felt. He spoke slowly but confidently, and made good eye contact. Gesturing for me to be seated, he lowered himself precariously onto the small metal chair opposite. Then he unbuttoned his jacket, loosened his tie and ran a meaty hand through an unruly thatch of graying hair. I wondered whether the tousled look was calculated. I had colleagues who beguiled witnesses into betraying confidences with a similar "aw, shucks" attitude.

Once we had settled ourselves around the table, the other detective spread out a thin manila folder, a notebook and pencil. Small, dark and sleek as a seal, the note-taker contrasted vividly with the interrogator. I noticed that no introductions were offered; I was left to guess at who was the senior man. Another tactic?

"O.K. to speak French?"

I nodded my assent. The big man smiled, his ruddy face collapsing into a contour map of lines and ridges, his eyes never leaving mine.

"Why are you here?"

I sighed, realizing that I would have to explain myself at length before I had any hope of getting *my* questions answered. Well, so be it. The details of who I was, Sam's relationship with Chantal, her disappearance, sounded rote to my ears now: the same vocabulary and phrasing from this morning's meeting with the curé, my conversation yesterday with Paulette, and the evening before that with Pierre: a well-rehearsed script for a drama whose next act was still a mystery.

"Is it her? Chantal, I mean? Was there any identification on the body?"

He smiled, leaving my questions unanswered.

"Why do you think it's Chantal Dubenoit?" He parried with his own question.

"Well, she lived here, then she disappeared. And it's her car, isn't it?"

"How do you know it's her car?"

I told him about Paulette and the information she had provided. The note-taker scribbled furiously.

"*Alors,* what else have you discovered about Mademoiselle Dubenoit?"

"Not much. You've been in her house. There's nothing much there." I hesitated. Should I share Paulette's theory, and Father Joseph's little nugget about Chantal wanting to work with children? If Chantal died here months ago, neither seemed relevant. I decided to try a different tack.

"Look, if the dead body is *not* Chantal, then Chantal is a missing person. Sam tried to report her missing to the police when he was here in April. Then, you said there was not enough evidence – she might have just been away on vacation. But now—"

The detective cut in.

"What does Mademoiselle Dubenoit look like?"

I remembered the photographs I still possessed. They were tucked into the notebook in my purse. I extracted them.

"This is the most recent. The other is perhaps twenty years old. That's her mother, Claire Dubenoit. She died last November."

"And the little girl in this other one?"

"Paulette Marsac's daughter."

He handed the photographs to his sidekick, who slipped them into his folder. They did not ask me where I had obtained them. Perhaps Pierre had already mentioned them. Probably this whole interview was just a repeat of Pierre's, an exercise in double-checking facts. But the detective's next question threw me.

"Was Chantal pregnant when she disappeared?"

"No! I mean, I don't know. Pierre's mother lived here and was perhaps the last person to see her, and she said nothing to Sam or Pierre about her being pregnant." I pictured the body in the car. In the brief moment before I backed away, I had not seen any obvious bulge, but it was dark and the corpse covered in what looked like an overcoat.

"The mother is dead, *n'est-ce pas*?"

"Yes, but the curé in St. Barthélemy knew Chantal too. He would have said something to us if he thought she was pregnant."

The other detective shut his notebook sharply, indicating the interview was over. My interrogator lumbered to his feet, fumbling in the pocket of his jacket. He had told me nothing!

"*Is* the woman in the car pregnant? How did she die? How long has she been dead?" I stumbled over my French in my desperation to get some answers.

The large man extended a business card to me, and gave another crinkly smile.

"We will know nothing for certain until after the autopsy. Please telephone in a day or two for more information. In the meantime," he leaned forward, wagging a finger at me as if I was a naughty child, "Do not assume, Mademoiselle, do not assume!"

With surprising speed, he and his partner trotted off around the corner of the building, leaving me staring at the small rectangle of white cardstock in my hand: *Dante Alighieri Parmentier, Inspecteur de Police.* His parents must have been big fans of medieval Italian poetry. No wonder he had failed to introduce himself.

***

"I'm still coming to France. I'll see you sometime on Sunday afternoon. I'm not giving up hope!" Sam's voice sounded firm and determined.

I was back in my room at the hotel; the ceiling fan whirred at full speed but was losing the battle against the late-day heat. I caught Sam during his lunch break at the Dispute Resolution Center. Perhaps he hadn't fully taken in what I had told him. I imagined him, at his cluttered desk, as I had so often seen him, a sandwich from the local deli shedding crumbs and grease stains onto file folders and legal pads, the phone wedged between ear and shoulder as he simultaneously took notes, searched for papers, and peered at the computer screen.

"The autopsy is tomorrow. The inspector said not to make any assumptions until we know more. At least now the police will take it seriously as a missing person's case, that is, if it's not ….." I trailed off, unwilling to verbalize – even in negative form – the most likely scenario: the body in the car was Chantal's. I changed the subject. "Have you heard from Dykstra?"

I was forced to admit I smarted from his failure to contact me since my arrival in France. I scolded myself that I set the parameters for our relationship, and shouldn't expect him to breach them, especially in the middle of a hectic book tour, but part of the yearning for home that had overwhelmed me earlier on Pierre's terrace was a yearning for *him;* a physical need to be held, to bury my face in his chest, to hear his voice in my ear. Just saying his name out loud to Sam sent a shiver through me, vulnerable as I was from the events of the afternoon.

"Only an e-mail confirming his flights. We'll meet up at Terminal 5 at Heathrow on Sunday morning, and fly on together to Bordeaux. He's somewhere on the West Coast, not sure where."

"O.K. I guess I'll e-mail him an update tonight."

But after I finished the call with Sam, I decided against getting online. I had not eaten all day, and my breakfast was lying in the weeds behind the barn at Le Bec. I needed sustenance, however exhausted I might feel, and the remains of the crackers I had picked up at the Spar yesterday would not suffice. My choices were the pizzeria and the restaurant offering *menus typiques de la région*. I washed my face, brushed my hair, and opted for a 'typical menu.'

This turned out to be duck, duck, goose, in various formats. Dordogne must be a nightmare for vegetarians. S*alade de gisiers* is by no stretch of the American imagination a salad: it consists of the parts that usually come in the little bag inserted into a fowl's cavity. I declined. The next course was *foie gras* which I recognized from my gourmet meal the night before, and enjoyed again, not being squeamish about the method farmers used to make the *foie* so deliciously *gras*. The main course was *magret du canard*, or duck breast: very tasty, with roast potatoes and green beans. By this time, half a bottle into a pleasant local red, I felt no pain. My thoughts wandered aimlessly, then homed in – inevitably – on Dykstra. I wondered what he was doing, checking my watch to work out the time difference. Did he think about me as he rushed from interview to book signing?

I am certain if there was a way to make dessert out of duck, the menu would have included it, but I was more than content with a selection of local cheeses and the rest of the bottle.

It was nine o'clock and still light when I made my unsteady way back to the Hotel Montbrun. Getting drunk over dinner may not be the adult way to deal with the shock of finding a dead body, but it beat an anxiety attack. Once in my room, I pulled out my laptop again and logged on, ready to write the e-mail to Dykstra that I had been composing in my head: *I miss you. I can't wait to see you. I've been thinking about you and how we can be together....*

The screen leaped into life, and there it was: an e-mail from him, subject line: *Missing you, can't wait to see you.* My tipsy-tiredness dropped away as I read on.

In San Francisco today, Seattle tomorrow, then back to London on Friday. Just time to do laundry and repack for the flight to Bordeaux with Sam on Sunday morning. We should be in St. Barthélemy by late afternoon. I long to be with you again, without the pressure of flights and meetings: just us, summertime, the French countryside!

I hit "reply." My fingers hovered over the keyboard. Sober now, I began to doubt my resolve to open up my heart to him. His words, into which I had at first read the passion *I* felt, now seemed merely friendly, as in: '*looking forward to spending some vacation time with you.*' It was never wise to commit in an e-mail; I should wait until we were together to gauge whether his feelings matched mine.

Re: Missing you, can't wait to see you
Me too.

Today, I found the dead body of a woman who may be Chantal in a barn at Le Bec ......

Chapter 12

France - Thursday

I slept badly, which is to say, not at all between one a.m. and sometime after dawn, when kitchen noises began to rise up from the lower regions of the old hotel. Then I fell hard into a dark dreamless place from which I woke sluggishly a little before nine. I hurriedly dressed and descended to the terrace before the breakfast buffet was cleared away.

Word travels fast in rural France. *Madame la Patronne*, who had served my coffee the previous day in decorous silence, bore down like a galleon under full sail when I emerged into the morning glare. She wasn't tall, but her suberb posture made her an imposing figure. That, and a certain Gallic arrogance.

"Shocking! Shocking! You must have been terrified! And poor Father Pierre: first his mother, then his neighbor! That place is cursed!" Without giving me a chance to protest that the body had not yet been identified, she turned to explain to an elderly British couple, the only other guests still at breakfast.

"Yesterday, Mademoiselle discovered a dead woman! Murdered!"

This was too much.

"No, the cause of death is not known yet. Neither is the identity of the … person." My head ached and my stomach roiled from the restless night, and possibly also from the excess of red wine consumed with dinner. I needed coffee, not a dramatic re-examination of yesterday's events.

The British couple leaned forward, abandoning the road map laid out in front of them, eyes wide, mouths agape.

"But my niece's husband – he works at the *Mairie* – he says the police told him--" Madame protested.

"They have to do an autopsy first," I said firmly. "By the way, do you know any children's homes in the country near here, perhaps in a castle?" Her blank look told me I had distracted her momentarily.

"No. Why do you ask?"

"Someone mentioned *la bastide*? I thought it might be the name of a house?"

Her face cleared.

"Yes, *La Bastide!* But it is not a house; it is a ruin. A crazy Swede bought it several years ago, and imported a dozen Polish workers to build a wall around it. We never see him. A very private man. His name is Hansen, I think."

"Can you tell me where it is?"

Madame pouted. She preferred to talk about murder. With a shrug, she turned back to the Brits.

"*Vous permettez?*" Without waiting for a response, she whipped the map out from under their astonished eyes, refolded it and indicated with her finger.

"Take the *Route Nationale* south towards Brantôme until you get to Pluviers. Then take this local road west to ….. Reilhac. See? After Reilhac, the road splits. Go left, perhaps a kilometer. La Bastide is on the left, there, but you won't see anything because of the wall, and you won't get inside. I told you, *very* private."

Smiling apologetically at the couple, I repatriated their map, and thanked Madame for the directions.

"Is there any coffee left?"

***

There was no obvious link between this reclusive Swede, Hansen, and Chantal Dubenoit, but I had nothing better to do while I waited for the autopsy results. I shot off another email to Sam and Dykstra about my plans to visit La Bastide.

The directions were easy to follow, and I had no trouble locating the wall, seven feet high, covered in dark grey stucco, topped with terra cotta tile, and completely out of place in this agricultural landscape of fields outlined by low dry-stone walls or wire fences. It must have cost a mint to build. I crept along in second gear looking for a name plate and gate. Nothing. After about three hundred yards, the wall disappeared into a copse of trees. I pulled over onto the grass verge and got out of the car to investigate. I could now see that the wall took a sharp right-angled turn and climbed up away from the road. I tried to follow along the outside of the wall, hoping, with an increase in elevation, to find a spot where I could look over into the property itself. After a few steps, I had to give up: the undergrowth, mainly thorn bushes, tore at my jeans and drew blood from my hands when I tried to part the branches.

I got back in the car and laboriously turned it around. The road was really no more than a roughly-paved lane wide enough for one vehicle. I started back the way I had come, scanning the wall again for anything I had missed. Every dozen or so yards, a small protuberance poked up from the tiled crest, the same pinky-brown as the tile, with a black circle a couple of inches wide on the side. It took me a minute to work out that these must be cameras, motion detectors, or some such security device. Impressive, and intriguing: what was so important to protect at such expense?

Now back at the spot where the wall started, I parked and strolled over to it. I had not noticed when I first passed this spot that this end of the wall was joined to a dilapidated metal shed with an overhead garage door facing onto the road. The door was plastered with a number of tattered notices: "*Proprieté Privé*," "*Défense d'Afficher*," some ancient legal notices, as well as an assortment of graffiti. I approached the side of the shed, hoping I could get behind it to discover the continuation of La Bastide's boundary, but again I was thwarted, this time by a stockade fence with rusty barbed wire along the top. There must be another access road on the other side of the estate, probably clearly marked and leading right up to the front door of the castle.

Wishing I had held onto the British couple's map, or purchased one for myself, I decided to try and find a way around to the front of La Bastide by taking repeated right turns. Failing that, I would surely see someone to ask for directions. My confidence in this plan drained over the next fifteen minutes, at the end of which I was completely lost and thoroughly confused, feeling like Alice in Wonderland, with not even a White Rabbit to point the way.

Tears of frustration misted my vision. What was happening to me? The slightest setback caused me to fall apart. Regardless of whether it was exhaustion, the remnants of jetlag, or just the loneliness of a stranger in a foreign land, I had better pull myself together before Sam and Dykstra arrived. Sam did not need to find me reduced to a pathetic hysteric. And Dykstra: if our re-connection was to take our relationship to a deeper level, I wanted it to be as equals, strong, independent adults choosing to be together. I cringed at the thought of him coming on all protective and macho, with me playing the helpless female. Echoes of last year's high seas adventure, a scenario I did not wish to repeat.

Then, unexpectedly, I spotted the sign for Reilhac. Somehow, I had made my way back to the village by a completely different route. I retraced my way to the main road and arrived back in St. Barthélemy by noon. The morning had been a colossal waste of time, but then I had nothing but time to waste. There would be no information from the autopsy yet.

Thank goodness, my room had already been made up. Things would look better after a nap.

***

The late afternoon heat woke me. I hadn't meant to sleep for quite so long, but I did feel better for it, and a long shower completed my recovery; I was used now to practicing a careful economy of movement in the narrow confines of the bathroom. I even contemplated a run, but decided instead to go for a stroll around the town.

The square bustled with activity. At one end, workmen in blue overalls were stacking planks and trusses for a temporary stage, between exchanging comments with locals gathered to watch and advise, and chasing off a gaggle of children intent on "helping." For the first time since I had arrived in St. Barthélemy, the big church doors stood wide open, a glorious noise of massed voices swelling out from the nave into the open air. It wasn't Sunday, or a feast day that I knew of. Intrigued, I crept into the dimness at the back of the church, and slid into a pew.

A choir was rehearsing: women and children mostly, but a few men as well, all dressed in their every-day clothes and ranged in rows on the steps in front of the altar. I couldn't recognize the songs, but it didn't sound like church music. I closed my eyes and let the beauty wash over me. When I opened them again and adjusted to the low light, I saw that several others had the same idea as me, and were enjoying the impromptu concert from scattered positions in the pews. Further towards the front, a couple of elderly women in black awaited their turn to enter a confessional booth. There was no sign of Father Joseph, for which I was grateful: his whirlwind energy would have destroyed the peace of the moment.

A figure made its way quietly, head bowed, down a side aisle towards the back of the church. With a thrill of pleasure, I recognized Pierre, and, as he passed behind me, I stood and followed him out into the sunshine.

"*Bonjour*, Pierre. What beautiful music!"

"Ah, *bonjour*, Sarah! Yes, they prepare for the *fête de musique*."

"A music festival? Here, in St. Barthélemy?"

"No, it's everywhere in France! Every year, on June 21st, the summer ... *comment dire?* ... solstice, there is a night of music. Everything from madrigals to garage bands, in churches, on the squares, in the parks. Look!" Pierre pointed to the stage under construction. "It's for *la fête de musique.*"

"That's wonderful! On Tuesday, right? My friends will be here then."

We stood for a moment watching the workers. I glanced sideways at Pierre's handsome profile. Although wings of longish dark hair hid his eyes, I had the impression that he was a little glum today.

"So, have you been to confession?" I meant it jokingly, but as soon as the words were out of my mouth, I regretted them. Pierre turned to me with an expression of such anguish, I thought he might burst into tears. "I'm so sorry—I didn't mean .... What is it, Pierre?"

"Yes, in a way I *was* making my confession. I met with Father Joseph finally. I told him about ... some things that happened in Canada. He is very disappointed, and I feel... sad." He sighed deeply, turning again to the activity at the other end of the square, but I doubted he was taking anything in. Abruptly, he faced me again.

"Shall we walk to the river?"

We set off down one of the cobbled streets that led out of the square, and quickly emerged onto the riverside path I had taken for my run two days earlier. There was a small park here with children's swings, and benches placed at intervals along the bank.

I remained silent, hoping Pierre would tell me more, but knowing all too well how a misplaced word might send him into retreat. He indicated a bench shaded by a giant sycamore, and we sat down, both of us keeping our gaze on the slow-moving water, green depths spangled with sunlight.

A minute passed before Pierre began to speak.

"The mission was in a remote village in Yukon Territory. First Nations people, at least until the mine opened. That brought in a lot of men. Young men without families. Nothing to do except work and drink. This girl, Rebekah, fourteen years old, daughter of one of the tribal leaders, very smart. I had such hopes for her; there were scholarships she could get .... Anyway, she got pregnant. I was the only one she told. Said it was a miner. I wanted to help her. I drove her down to Prince Rupert, left her there at a women's shelter. I thought she'd be safe …." He took a deep breath; hands clenched into fists on his knees. "Her father found out, dragged her back. He came to mass and denounced me in front of the congregation, said I had seduced her, wrote to the archdiocese too. I was removed and reassigned to serve as chaplain at a prison in Montreal, pending an investigation. I had been there three weeks when someone wrote to say Rebekah had … hanged herself. She left a note. It wasn't a mine worker that got her pregnant; it was her own father." Pierre's voice swelled with remembered outrage. He calmed himself and resumed in a subdued, bitter voice.

"When I heard, I was so filled with rage. I wanted to …. Well, I wrote letters. To everyone I could think of, but it did nothing. There was nothing to be done. Rebekah was dead. The tribe closed ranks, and so did the Church. Then my mother died, and I had an excuse to escape, to run away … give up."

He turned to me, his intense brown eyes filled with tears.

"I can't be a priest anymore. I don't *want* to be a priest anymore, but telling Father Joseph—" He stood up and took a step towards the river. For a split second, I feared he was going to throw himself in.

"What will you do now?" I wanted to distract him, pull him away from his pain.

He shrugged.

"I don't know. Teach, maybe. Isn't that what disgraced priests do?" he said sourly.

At that moment, my cell phone rang. It had been so long – actually, only a few days ago in Atlanta – since I had heard the little jazz riff selected from the tones offered, that I was momentarily confused, looking around for the source. I didn't expect any calls, having warned my contacts that I would be away from the office, overseas and many time zones away, and having arranged with Sam and Dykstra to communicate by e-mail. When I managed to dig the phone out from the bottom of my shoulder bag, the screen announced a French area code. My first instinct was to dismiss the call – it seemed so insensitive to Pierre who was still standing a pace away staring gloomily into the river – but then I thought that it might be Inspector Parmentier with news from the autopsy.

"*Allo?*"

"Sarah! *C'est moi,* Paulette! The dead one! She is not Chantal!"

"What?" I had forgotten that I had given Paulette Marsac my cell phone number as well as my e-mail address. Her penetrating voice reached Pierre; he looked inquiringly at me. "You have the autopsy results?"

"*Quoi? Non! L'inspecteur*, he comes to ask me, and I tell him it is not possible it is Chantal."

"But how do you know?" My voice was rising in pitch to match hers.

"Chantal is not *enceinte*, er, pregnant, when I see her in *décembre*, and the dead one is – pouf! – very big, he tell me. Not possible. But the hairs show it better. You remember the photo of Chantal and my little Francine? The hairs of Chantal are short, *n'est-ce pas?*" I thought back; Paulette was right: Chantal's hair in the image was short, barely covering her ears.

"The dead one has the long hairs. Very long, *l'inspecteur* says this. Not possible to grow so long in a few months. A few years, *peut-être*." She laughed triumphantly. I forced my mind back to my shadowy glimpse of the corpse in the car: luxuriant dark hair that contrasted with the pallor of a ruined face; hair that swept down well below the shoulders of the black garment cloaking the torso. I felt a flush of relief run through me: Chantal was alive! At least, she was not the dead body sitting in the car in the barn.

"But then who is the dead woman?"

Paulette made the "pfft" sound of blowing air through pursed lips.

"I don't know. But it is not Chantal!"

I hurriedly thanked her and terminated the call, with promises to keep her informed of anything *I* could find out about the mystery dead woman or Chantal's whereabouts.

As I summarized the call for Pierre, I struggled with how to – or even whether to – return to the story he had just told me. I had an urge to hug him, stroke his hair, and comfort him. He seemed so young in some ways, and so vulnerable. I knew better than to give in to my impulse. He was listening to me now with a pleasantly interested expression, and the wounded look was gone from his eyes. I would respect the veil of politeness drawn over his pain.

"I need to call Inspector Parmentier," I told Pierre. "If the dead woman is not Chantal, the police have got to take her disappearance seriously now." I fished Dante Aligheri's card out of my wallet, and started dialing the phone number into my phone.

"Do you want me to speak to him?" Pierre offered. Yes, that made sense. I could handle conversational French face-to-face, but on the phone without visual cues it was much harder. Even face-to-face, my track record on getting information from Parmentier was not good. The man-to-man thing couldn't hurt either. I handed Pierre the phone, and stood as close to his side as I felt was proper so I could try to hear what the inspector said. However, although I followed Pierre's polite but insistent questions, the detective's responses were too rapid for me to understand.

"Well? What did he say?" I asked as Pierre handed back my phone.

"He said the dead woman is not Chantal Dubenoit. There is a possible match with a woman who went missing last year from the La Rochelle area. No name until the identity is confirmed and they can talk to the family. The cause of death is still unknown, although he did say the body was malnourished, even though she was in the third trimester of pregnancy."

"Do they know when she died?"

"About nine weeks ago, he said."

That would date her death to late April, about the time Sam visited Le Bec, and shortly before Pierre's mother died. Of course, the body could have been placed in the barn at a later time, maybe even after Pierre returned to France. I set aside the mystery of the woman's death and returned to Chantal.

"Are the police doing anything to find Chantal?"

"The inspector said he had all the information from Paulette Marsac about Chantal's bank, e-mail and cell phone, and was 'following it up.' "

"Hmm. Hey, we should tell him what Father Joseph said about her going to work for a child rescue organization. When he interviewed me yesterday, I didn't say anything because I thought Chantal was ... the body in the barn." I shivered again at the memory.

"O.K. Give me your phone again."

Pierre spent a few minutes explaining who the curé was and how he came to know Chantal's plans. The inspector's response was brief.

"He said he'd look into it." Pierre's expression indicated his suspicion – and mine – that the priorities of the inspector with the romantic name lay elsewhere than with a possible missing person case.

Chapter 13

France – Thursday - Friday

The church clock struck six-thirty as we arrived back in the square. The workers had knocked off for the evening, and the usual pre-dinner *passaggio* was taking place: elderly locals commandeered the benches, children chased each other noisily around the fountain, and a group of older children huddled over illicit cigarettes in the shade of the largest tree. The two cafés were doing good business.

I experienced a strange mix of emotions. Above all, I was relieved that it wasn't Chantal's body in the barn. Yes, she was still missing, but at least the police were now involved, and could bring their resources to bear in the search. Access to her bank records might be key to tracking her movements. I would just have to keep the pressure on Inspector Parmentier, or whoever the police assigned to the case. At the same time, the image of the dead woman haunted me. I couldn't shake the horror I felt when the mouse ran up her arm and disappeared inside her clothes. Or the smell: the memory inhabited my nostrils still. Who was she, and how did she end up at Le Bec?

My sympathy for Pierre pulsed under these other feelings. He had lost, in short order, his position, his protégée, his mother, and his vocation – perhaps even his faith. Even though I had known him for only a few days, and our backgrounds differed tremendously, I felt his pain. Our shared experience of finding the body, as well as the help he volunteered in the search for Chantal, bound me to him. I was nervous about encroaching on his privacy, but wanted to acknowledge the honor he paid me in confiding his story.

We came to a halt outside the church. I put a hand on his arm.

"Pierre, thank you for telling me about Canada. I'm so sorry for everything that happened."

Pierre looked at my hand, and for one awful moment I thought he might push it away. Then he covered it briefly with his own and smiled, before moving off again across the square.

"Pizza?" He asked over his shoulder. He pronounced it the French way: *'peedsa.'* "They have a wood-fired oven, it's quite good."

"I'd love to!" I ran to catch up with him.

We were halfway through a large 'mushroom with four cheeses,' and I was turning over in my head the information gleaned from Dante Aligheri. What was the link between a woman from La Rochelle and Le Bec? What if both she and Chantal's car arrived *together* at the barn? Perhaps she knew Chantal, and drove the car back to Le Bec at her request? Or maybe she had died elsewhere, and some third party had ferried the body *and* the car back to the barn? Why? Did Pierre's mother know something? Had she seen something – or someone – suspicious? Had they seen her?

"Pierre, exactly how did your mother die?"

He looked at me quizzically for a moment, before succinctly laying out the facts. The curé found Madame Albert on Monday, April 25, in the morning. He had missed her at mass the day before, and drove out to Le Bec in his beat-up Renault to check on her. She was sitting in her favorite chair, eyes closed and hands folded over the open pages of a magazine. The curé called the doctor, who examined her and determined she had died some time the previous day of heart failure. There was no sign of struggle or trauma. She had no history of heart disease, but she was nearly seventy years old.

"You think her death was ... unnatural?" Pierre asked. His hand, laden with the final slice of pizza, stopped on its way to his mouth.

"No! ...I don't know! I'm trying to think why a pregnant woman from a hundred miles away is found dead in Chantal's car at Le Bec. I thought your mother might know something about Chantal's disappearance. Is it possible she *did* know something, maybe about the dead woman, and was silenced?"

Pierre shook his head slowly. He put down the pizza.

"No, Sarah. People die. My mother was old. She just died. It was peaceful. Please, don't ... make a drama of this."

I was stung by his words. I was *not* being dramatic. There was a mystery here, and if Pierre was too wrapped up in his own tragic story to see the possibility that his mother had paid the price of being a witness to a crime, then *I* would pursue the matter. It took less than a second to see how ridiculous that sounded. Perhaps I *was* over-reacting as a result of my raw emotional state. After all, there was not a shred of evidence that Madame Albert had been murdered. We didn't even know the cause of death of the body in the car yet, although murder seemed probable. I was just a foreigner here with few resources to investigate a crime, other than the man who sat opposite me. The man who, one moment, warmly drew me in, and, the next, distanced himself with a cool phrase.

We finished the meal in near-silence, and split the bill. It took less than five minutes to walk back to the square where we parted company, our goodnights sounding formal. I made my way back to the hotel, swathed in self-pity, feeling more alone than at any time since I had arrived in France. I broke my resolution and took a sleeping pill. The last thing I needed was another night of tossing and turning, soured by self-reproach.

***

I did not escape recrimination, however. When I woke on Friday morning, my brain was clogged with a chemical hangover. Through the fog came the realization I had not let Sam and Dykstra know of the latest development: Chantal was not the body in the barn. In fact, I had not logged onto my laptop for almost thirty-six hours! What kind of a sleuth was I?

I rapidly composed an e-mail bringing Sam and Dykstra up to date. They would be asleep by now on the East and West Coasts of America, but at least they'd have good news to greet them when they rose; Sam, to face a last day at the Center, beavering to get everything squared away before his trip; Dykstra, to embark on a long day and night of travel back to London.

After pressing "send," I quickly scanned the subject lines of a dozen new messages, so quickly that I almost missed it: a reply from Chantal! With suddenly shaky fingers, I opened it. The message was dated two days before, in French, and brief.

Dear Sarah:
I am happy that my father is coming to France. My work keeps me very busy, but if it is convenient, I can meet you in Brantôme on Friday at 11:00 at the café in the park by the river. Please confirm.
Chantal Dubenoit

It was already eight o'clock. *Yes! I'll be there.* My excitement banished all remaining grogginess. Not only was Chantal alive, she was still in Dordogne, and I was going to see her in just three hours! After the ups and downs of the last five days, this denouement presented itself with such simplicity and ease, I could hardly believe it. I re-read Chantal's e-mail slowly, looking for the catch, the give-away that this was a fake, some imposter's trick, but although the text was spare, it contained no false notes. My only question was whether Chantal would receive my confirmation in time. If she found no reply before she left for work, she might not check her emails again, and therefore not keep the appointment in the park. I would just have to hope. I forwarded Chantal's message to Sam and Dykstra, together with my response: more good news to wake up to back home.

From my excursion the day before, I knew Brantôme was fifty kilometers south, less than an hour's drive. The picturesque town, centered on an island created by an oxbow sweep of the Dronne river, drew busloads of tourists in the summer. Google Maps showed me an impenetrable tangle of narrow streets on the island itself, but there seemed room to park on the north side of town. The "park by the river" Chantal had chosen was clearly indicated across a bridge leading south from the center.

The weather was auspicious: another cloudless summer morning, a slight breeze moving through the trees, and the promise of later heat. I showered and dressed carefully in a sleeveless flower-print dress with a gathered skirt, strappy sandals. After nine months, the scars on my upper arm looked like nothing more than a botched inoculation; I went sleeveless as a minor act of defiance. With my hair pulled back into a pony tail and tied with a blue bandanna, the effect could be summed up as: '*Audrey Hepburn, girl detective.*' Making sure my big shoulder bag contained sunscreen, sunglasses, water bottle, a fully-charged phone, and my notebook, I descended to breakfast, planning to leave without returning to my room. I found myself too nervous to relish the breakfast buffet, although I had ample time to eat. Instead, I downed a cup of coffee while reducing a croissant to sticky flakes.

Madame's source at the *Mairie* had been unable to come up with any more information on the dead body, which she now grudgingly admitted was *not* Chantal Dubenoit. I wasn't sure what instinct prevented me from disclosing to Madame that indeed Chantal was very much alive and I was on my way to meet her. Perhaps it was plain contrariness that led me to deny her the information, but I rationalized that her track record for spreading distorted versions of the facts inspired my reluctance to share. I mumbled something about checking out the sights in Brantôme and made my escape.

Of course, I still had nearly an hour to spare by the time I secured my parking spot in the lot on the way into the town. I decided to stroll through the center, before crossing the bridge to the park on the south bank of the Dronne. On any other day, I would have delighted in the ancient little town, its winding streets and inviting boutiques. Cafés and restaurants claimed the prime spots on the exterior, their patios and balconies leaning precariously over the rushing water. I learned from the brochure I picked up at *l'Office de Tourisme* that Brantôme's abbey had been a stop on the pilgrimage route to Santiago de Compostela in the Middle Ages. The current abbey, rebuilt several times, presented an imposing but rather bland façade wedged up against the cliff on the other side of the river. It had been secularized during the French Revolution.

It was still early for the tour buses, and the narrow streets were pleasantly shaded. Forcing myself to look in every shop window and examine every posted menu, I managed to delay my arrival at the park until ten-thirty. The café was an al fresco affair: a dozen tables surrounding a kiosk whose open side revealed a well-stocked bar, beer pumps and the inevitable espresso machine. I ordered a *café allongé* – all this caffeine was doing nothing to calm my nerves – and sat back to survey my surroundings.

The café was situated at the meeting point of three graveled paths, each bordered by flower beds dancing with summer colors. The central one – the one I had used -- led back to the bridge to the island-center of Brantôme. The one on my left went to a lovely old mill and a narrower bridge over to the abbey side of the Dronne. On my right, the path ended at a gate onto a busy road leading south out of town. Children played on the grassy lawns, but the paths were uncrowded. I was well-placed to monitor Chantal's approach.

Ten-forty-five. I gave up the pretense of studying the tourist brochure, and attempted to prepare myself for the interview with Chantal. She had not seen Sam for thirty years. She might have dreamed up – or been fed by her mother – a completely wrong idea of who her father was. Who knew what her expectations were? I needed to be absolutely non-threatening. I should invite her questions, not volunteer too much information. My job was to pave the way for father and daughter to establish a relationship based on the present, not mired in the guilt and betrayals of the past. This meeting was the first step on a long road.

I resisted turning my phone on to check for messages. My data plan for Europe was very restricted, and, outside the haven of the hotel's wi-fi zone, going online was ruinously expensive, assuming, of course, I was even in an area with service. Either she would turn up or she wouldn't. At least she'd made contact. There was time to set up another meeting over the weekend if necessary. I wondered if her work schedule allowed weekends off. Sam was arriving on Sunday. If all went well, I might arrange a family reunion over Sunday dinner.

Eleven o'clock. I moved to another table with more shade, taking the opportunity to circumnavigate the whole café area to make sure that I had not missed another hidden section where Chantal might be waiting.

Eleven-ten. Fashionably late, or had she missed my responsive e-mail?

Eleven-twenty. The café was getting crowded, and I felt pressure to order another drink. Expense be damned, I unlocked my phone and updated my email in-box. Nothing. No voicemails or missed calls either. I scanned the pathways for the umpteenth time: no forty-ish woman on her own who resembled the person in the photo I had taken from Chantal's bedroom. No solitary women at all; everyone seemed paired up or in a group of friends.

Eleven-thirty.

"Excuse me, but are you by any chance Sarah McKinney?"

I had not noticed his approach, fixated as I was with looking for Chantal. Medium height, brown hair receding into widow's peaks, and watery eyes behind rimless glasses. His crooked-toothed smile was tentative, his English slightly accented. I immediately thought of the illustration of a mouse in a long-ago children's picture book. Or was it Ratty in *Wind in the Willows*? I nodded and waited.

"My name is Thomas Schiffer. Doctor Schiffer. I was coming to Brantôme anyway so Chantal asked me to find you. She works with me at the ... Er, she's been delayed..." He looked over his shoulder. His voice tailed off. It appeared to require an effort to meet my eye. "May I sit down?"

"Yes, of course. She did say her work kept her very busy. What exactly is her position at the, er ....?" I copied his hesitant diction, hoping to draw him out. I was disappointed not to be asking the question directly to Chantal, but perhaps this setback was not entirely unfortunate: I would be better prepared to approach Chantal if I more clearly understood her present situation.

"Oh, she's essential! The children love her! Some of them come to us so badly damaged, but she has wonderful patience. That's why she isn't here. One of the little girls experienced a crisis. Only Chantal can calm her."

"Ah, I see..." Not seeing much at all. "And what is your role at the ...er...?"

He looked surprised that I didn't know.

"I'm the director, a psychologist by training, but we're a small staff; we all help."

"How long has Chantal been there?"

"About three months, I think." He suddenly clapped a hand to his jacket pocket. I hadn't heard the phone ring, perhaps it was set on vibrate mode. He drew it out and stood up.

"Will you excuse me for a minute?" He paced off a few yards and stood hunched over with his back to me. I couldn't hear what he said. He returned to the table with a frown on his face. "That was Chantal. She is not able to join you here today. The patient is sleeping now, but very restless. Chantal feels she cannot leave the building."

"Oh, dear," I was frustrated, but still not hopeless. "Perhaps ... would it be possible for me to go to her? I don't want to disrupt your work, but if I could just talk to her for a few minutes? Her father is arriving on Sunday. They haven't seen each other for many years. I wanted a chance to prepare her ..." And gather information to prepare Sam, too.

Dr. Schiffer pondered my request, chin on chest, hands fiddling with the cell phone.

"Miss McKinney, we keep the location of the Home secret for good reason. Our patients have been the victims of the most terrible abuse. Their families, communities, the law, social services – all have failed them. Their safety – their *perception* of safety – depends on keeping them isolated." He sighed, looking away from me at the happy children playing on the grass that sloped down to the river.

"But I could meet her in private? In your office, perhaps?" I sensed he was weakening.

"Mmm. Well, I suppose it might be possible," He looked at his watch. "Where are you parked?"

I described the parking lot on the other side of the center.

"All right, go to your car. I'll meet you there with my car, and then you can follow me to the Home. I'll give you directions in case we get separated."

"Thank you!"

It was only as I was dashing back through the center of town that I began to question the wisdom of following a stranger to an unknown destination. Dr. Schiffer seemed harmless enough, with his mousey looks and hesitant speech, but I had not seen any identification proving he was indeed Chantal's boss. But how else could he have obtained the information about our meeting? And if I suspected he was leading me astray as we caravanned away from Brantôme, I would be in my own car. I could peel off and escape, and contact Chantal again later.

I lowered the car windows to let the heat escape, then fished my phone out of my shoulder bag, praying for service. The least I could do was let someone know where I was and what I was doing. I regretted keenly that Pierre had no cell phone, and had not shared his e-mail address with me, if he even had one. Instead, I tapped out a message for Sam and

Dykstra, explaining that Chantal had not been able to meet me as arranged, and I was going to follow this Dr. Schiffer, the director of the Children's Home where Chantal worked, in my car. As I hit send, I glanced in the mirror and saw a black SUV draw up behind my spot, obstructing my exit. I fumbled the phone, trying to put it back in my bag, and it fell into the narrow gap between the two front seats. Never mind, I would retrieve it later. I turned, aiming to climb out of the car and confront Dr. Schiffer face-to-face, but he was already at the car door. He had an unfolded road map in his hands.

"Let me show you where the Home is." He reached in the open window, awkwardly spreading the map across the steering wheel and my chest like a bib. "Here."

Before I could focus on the section he was indicating, I felt a sharp pain in my upper arm. I turned my head to see Schiffer withdraw a hypodermic syringe through the window.

"What are you doing?" Even as I spoke the words, my mouth filled with cotton. The map seemed to float up like mist and settle over me, blocking sound, vision, all my senses. My last conscious thought was how stupid I had been.

Chapter 14

France – Friday continued

I floated just below the surface of consciousness. A garage door closed. Such a familiar sound that I relaxed down again into oblivion: I was home, in my garage, safe....

Minutes or hours later, I swam up into full awareness. Stifling hot, swathed in something dark, seated with my arms constricted, my legs flailing. Panic clawed at my lungs. I twisted my head from side to side in a desperate attempt to see a seam of light, anything my senses might recognize, anything I could seize on to orient myself. Memories of the horrors of the previous Fall rushed into my mind like flood water: the pain of plastic ties cutting into my wrists and the acrid odor of burned flesh, all this triggering a deeper memory, a body-memory of darkness and restraint, a child's nightmare of smothering under an unbearable weight, unable to escape. A bad dream where every movement seemed mired in quicksand, every attempt at speech stifled before I opened my lips. Without any outside sensory information, I began to drown in my own terror, incapable of thinking rationally ... of thinking at all.

I don't know what remnant of self-control dragged my mind back from the brink. Probably some unconscious echo of the anti-anxiety techniques I had studied so assiduously when I was younger and striving to reinvent myself as calm and competent. I focused all my effort on breathing in and out. In and out. After I managed to slow my respiration to a more normal rate, I admonished myself that I had survived those earlier ordeals, and would this, if I could just exercise some discipline and not succumb to fear. The next step in this ad hoc self-help program was to marshal the facts. I couldn't hope to change the situation unless I understood it.

So I stopped struggling, and listened hard. At first, I heard only the pounding of blood through my veins. No, there was something else: the faint whirr of machinery, distant fans maybe, and along with that recognition, the sensation of cool air on my arms. Then, a sound. Footsteps on a hard floor.

"I'm going to take the hood off now." My heart jumped into my throat; the voice was so unexpectedly close. Thomas Schiffer's? I thought so, but now in a lower register and without the tentative hesitations that had characterized his speech when we met in the park. I reared away from a touch at my neck. Then the thick material lifted off my face, and I blinked in the sudden brightness.

He stood in front of me, his eyes level with mine, his pale face expressionless. I glanced down. The chair I was bound to at the wrists with duct tape and at the waist with a webbing strap, was elevated, the kind of rolling office chair used by architects at a raised desk. My legs dangled childishly a foot above the floor. I looked around, not prepared yet to trust my voice. The room was large, with a high beamed ceiling, stone floor and whitewashed rough stone walls. Except for the chair I was sitting in, there was no furniture in the central part of the room, but ranged along the wall ahead of me were computer screens, at least a half-dozen large flat-screen monitors and a couple of open laptops. Metal boxes I guessed to be hard drives stood underneath the broad shelf on which the monitors sat. Box fans – yes, I had been right – blew cool air over the complete array. White shades covered narrow windows in deep embrasures. The door must be behind me, but I could not turn my neck back far enough to verify this.

I returned my gaze to Thomas Schiffer, deciding to wait him out as I took stock of my physical state. My head was still pounding with the residue of whatever knock-out drug he had given me and my mouth felt like the floor of a parrot's cage, but otherwise I seemed uninjured or "interfered with" as my former sponsor Miss Mumford would say: my dress draped demurely over my knees, my feet still shod in the flimsy sandals I had chosen that morning. Whatever this man wanted from me was yet to emerge. Schiffer's expression was unnervingly blank.

It *was* Schiffer, although there were subtle changes in his appearance, just as there were in his voice. I had dismissed his eyes as pale and watery before, but now, without the rimless glasses he had worn in the park, they were the color of tempered steel. His hairline was different: the widow's peaks now covered by a comb-over.

"Who have you told about the appointment in Brantôme today?"

I took a deep breath. This was the moment to call on the skills I had honed over years of mediating conflict: listen for the underlying interests, affirm the speaker's concerns, invite him to suggest solutions. All good in a conference room with civilized disputants dressed in business suits; hard to practice when immobilized in some madman's lair. But I knew my best hope lay in creating some kind of link with him, getting inside his defenses to understand his motives. Here goes.

"You must be worried about my friends coming to find me. Look, you're in control here, obviously, but if you don't want trouble, you could just let me go now. Just take me back to my car. I'll wear the hood again if you want." I managed with difficulty to keep my voice even, my expression neutral.

He shook his head, frowning. He remained intimidatingly close to me. I saw sweat beading his pale upper lip. I could smell it too. A sign of stress or just poor grooming? I schooled myself not to lean away from him, to keep eye contact.

"Where is your mobile phone?"

As he spoke, I noticed another difference. Before, his teeth had been large, crooked and stained; now they were small, white and even. The teeth, the glasses and the hairstyle – probably the name – were all part of a disguise he had adopted for the meeting in the park. Who *was* this man, and what connection did he have with Chantal?

"I don't know," I responded. Then I remembered. My phone had fallen between the front seats of the rental car. Schiffer – or whoever he was -- had probably grabbed my bag when he grabbed me, and searched it for the device that tracked all my recent communications. I tried to steer him away from that line of inquiry. "Is Chantal here?"

He didn't answer but a tell-tale sideways flicker of his eyes towards the computers gave me another question.

"Do you have her laptop? Is that how you knew about the meeting? No!" Suddenly, it was clear. "You set it up; you replied to my e-mail! Is she here? Is she OK?"

His shoulders twitched nervously, and his gaze drifted away from me. I sneaked an instinctive look at my wrist but my watch was covered by the tape that secured me to the arms of the chair. How long had I been here? Long enough for Sam and Dykstra to wonder why I had not reported on my meeting with Chantal? But they were half a world away. What good would it do, even if they were concerned? No one else knew about my trip to Brantôme except Madame at the hotel, and it would take at least a day before she realized that I was missing.

I had to get him talking. His staccato questions, and silence in response to mine, were not getting me anywhere.

"Tell me what you need me to do. Maybe we can work something out. I'm just interested in finding out about Chantal. If you tell me what you know, I promise I won't make problems for you about …. all this." I indicated my restraints with an inclined head.

He looked at me reflectively, then extended a finger, trailing a line slowly from my ear lobe down my throat, hooking the scooped neckline of my dress so that my upper body was jerked forwards. *Tell me what you need me to do.* Oh God, had I implied I'd have sex with this freak? I sealed my lips together to prevent any other idiocies emerging, and pulled back against his hand. His eyes which had been wandering over my body like a snail's trail, reverted to my face. Suddenly, he let go of my dress and slapped me hard across the cheek. The sting brought tears to my eyes and forced a whimper through my closed lips.

"You!" He spat the word out. "I need nothing from you! You're just a trouble-maker, poking around where you don't belong!" Well, at least I had got him talking, shouting actually, his pallor suddenly suffused with crimson blotches. "I've been watching you—"

He broke off, sputtering, as the light dawned: I was inside La Bastide, the walled estate with the high-tech security, that I had failed to penetrate yesterday. I peered over at the bank of computer screens again. I could make out that three of the larger screens were quartered. Several of the twelve resulting mini-screens showed a different angled view over what looked like a country road, probably the road that skirted the perimeter. That was what he meant by "watching" me. This man must be Hansen, the eccentric Swede with a penchant for privacy. Had he lured me to Brantôme and then kidnapped me to punish me for my nosiness, or to frighten me into minding my own business, his paranoid need for absolute privacy driving him to criminal acts? That didn't explain the connection to Chantal, or how he had been able to access her e-mail account to reply to my message.

His abrupt descent into rage cautioned me to keep quiet. This man was not rational. Any hope that I could negotiate my way to freedom drained away. I would have to find a way to escape. I just needed to be patient and observant. Surely, at some point he would untie me, and that might offer an opportunity to overpower him, or distract him, or ….. The futility of my planning swept over me. I was helpless. This time, I could not hope that some *deus ex machina* would arrive to save me, like the sudden appearance of the FBI agent on the yacht *Glissando* last year.

Hansen paced in front of me. Then, grabbing the chair, he spun it around and pushed it roughly forward. My teeth knocked together and the strap at my waist cut into my diaphragm, pushing my breath out. For a sickening moment, I thought I would crash to the floor, unable to protect my head from impact on the hard stone, but the chair rolled to a stop just short of a heavy oak door, banded in metal. Hansen came up behind me, and again I tensed, anticipating more violence. He could ram the chair against the closed door, crushing my kneecaps and my immobilized knuckles. But he seemed to have recovered a measure of self-control. He opened the door and pushed me through into a dark corridor.

The fieldstone walls, crevices filled with coarse mortar, confirmed that I was in a castle. Here, no whitewash or translucent blinds added grace notes of modernity. As Hansen hurried me over the uneven floor, I caught glimpses of the sky through arrow-slit openings in the upper part of the left-hand wall: still blue, but not the luminous color of midday; now, the sky glowed with the deepening indigo of a midsummer evening. I struggled to remember whether the moon would be full tonight, then almost laughed at the irrelevance of my thought. A moonlit escape through romantic woods was improbable. I reminded myself to concentrate on the here and now, and gather as much information about my situation and my captor's intentions as I could.

The corridor sloped down past a closed door on the right. The chair bumped down a few steps, which pushed out a startled yell from me. There were no more windows, and, after the corridor twisted leftwards, little light. Hansen did not reduce his speed. He was humming quietly, something tuneless but repetitive, in time to the sound of the castors on the rough stone floor. I licked my lips, and started to phrase a question, more to reassure myself that I still had a voice than in any hope of a response. He forestalled me.

"Keep quiet."

We stopped suddenly. I could just make out a recess in the wall at my side. It measured about four feet in height and three in width. Hansen crouched forward and I heard the sound of a bolt withdrawn and the squeak of ancient hinges. He paused, listening, his head hidden in the opening. If the chair had been turned towards him, I could have aimed a kick that might have sent him crashing through the little door, but before I could work out how to turn the chair, he stood up again. He had a kitchen knife in his hand.

"Don't! Please …" All my resolution to stay calm fled in a second. "Please …" I squeezed my eyes shut and braced for his thrust, but all I felt was a cool lick of steel at my wrists as he slid the knife under the duct tape to slice me free. I stared in amazement as he performed the same operation on the other side, then moved around me to release the strap that secured me to the chair at my waist.

"Now, in there." He gestured with the knife towards the dwarf door.

Abruptly, one terror replaced another.

"I can't! It's too small! There's no light. Please …" I hated to hear the craven whining in my voice, but I couldn't help myself. How had he devised this customized torture for me? How had he known my profound fear of being trapped in a small dark place?

He laid the blade flat against my cheek, the point towards my eye. With his other hand he yanked me off the chair. I cowered away from him, momentarily more scared of being blinded than imprisoned. He twisted me around, the knife now pricking the back of my neck, and pushed me savagely towards the recessed door. I ducked to avoid my skull crashing into the stone lintel, and felt myself propelled into space. I heard the door bang shut behind me, a heavy bolt shooting home as I sprawled on the dirt floor of the cell, winded by my fall.

Gasping, I made it to all fours, but no further. My head hung forward between my arms, eyes squeezed shut against the stinging pain in palms and knees. My gasps turned to sobs, as I finally broke down completely. So this was how it would end for me. After escaping the alternating neglect and violence of my childhood, and toiling for so many years to achieve an education, a career, a new persona in a new country, I was back where I began: confined, forgotten and alone. I thought bitterly of my perfect little home in Decatur, of the countless hours I had spent creating the illusion of security with paint and plaster. I thought of the law school class I would now never teach. My sobs redoubled when I thought of Sam and his touching but totally misplaced confidence in my ability to find Chantal and effect a reconciliation between them. Dykstra had been right: I was an arrogant fool to think I could come to France and solve the mystery like some heroine in a cheap thriller from an airport bookstand. I had come to believe the deception I practiced on the rest of the world, the sleight of hand that created the impression of competence. Now, stripped bare of artifice, I was again the skinny kid in a dirty dress, sniveling in a corner.

My orgy of self-pity and recrimination was winding down when I heard a rustle that brought me to my feet in renewed panic: rats! I was going to share my final hours with the creatures I dreaded most! I looked around wild-eyed, realizing that the cell was not, after all, completely dark. Maybe ten feet up in one wall, a barred opening showed the twilight sky. By its light, I made out the dimensions of my prison, a space about eight feet square. A wide bench stretched from wall to wall at sitting height; perhaps it had offered a rudimentary bed for prisoners long ago. Or maybe not so long ago: the stone walls exuded a strong smell of decay overlaid with something sharper that caught at the back of my throat. Dead rat? I heard the noise again; it came from the shadows underneath the bench. Live rat eating dead rat?

I backed away, watching in horror as the shadows seemed to move and grow, edging out and across the floor towards me. Then, suddenly, a human face emerged, surrounded by dark, matted hair. The features were grimy and marked by tear tracks; the eye sockets looked bruised, the eyes themselves bloodshot.

"Ne me faites pas du mal, je vous en prie!" The voice was husky, a croak that did not reveal the gender of the speaker crouching in front of me, but although she looked nothing like the images I had seen, I knew who it was.

"Chantal!"

Chapter 15

France – Friday to Saturday

"Ne me touchez pas!"

Fearing rats, I had backed away almost into the recess that housed the door. Now, I stepped forward again, but Chantal extended her arm, palm outwards to ward me off.

I paused, trying to summon up the words in French that would reassure her that I was a friend.

"My name is Sarah. I'm an American, a friend of your father's. Chantal, I am so happy to see you. We have been worried. Are you O.K.? " I didn't want to confuse her with the news that her long-estranged father had sent me to find her, and I didn't approach any closer but waited while she digested my words. She clambered painfully to her feet, and stood unsteadily peering at me. She presented a pitiful sight, clutching a blanket around her shoulders with a dirty, claw-like hand, her face gaunt, mouth working, eyes glassy with terror. Even from a few feet away, I could smell the sharp mix of dried sweat and fear.

"Did he...." She swallowed painfully before resuming. "Did he send you here? What more does he want?" Her voice was a cracked whisper; speaking appeared to hurt her. At least she dropped her arm, and did not retreat under the bench again.

"Hansen? No! He captured me too, because I was trying to find you." I wondered how long Chantal had been imprisoned in this twilit hell-hole, and when she had last eaten or drunk anything. I was uncertain how much information she could take in. She was shivering, although the cell was a comfortable temperature. She stumbled backwards, landing clumsily on the bench. I edged forward and sat down, leaving a few feet between us, and keeping my body turned away a little, so as not to seem threatening.

"You know my father?"

"Yes. Sam Cantor. After he learned that your mother had died, he wanted to .... renew your relationship." The French phrases sounded coldly formal. "He knows you are alone and he wants to help you. He came to Le Bec in April but you were already gone. He comes to France again on Sunday. I came in advance to find you."

Chantal's eyes searched my face as she again labored to clear her throat.

"But now you are a prisoner too. How ....?" Her croaking whisper trailed off. She did not need to complete the question: how could Sam help her now that we were both buried in this oubliette?

Strangely, the despair that had disabled me minutes before dissolved. Finding Chantal gave me new energy. Perhaps the responsibility for keeping her spirits up distracted me from the situation, which was just as dire as it was before. Fleetingly, I remembered that Chantal had witnessed my miserable display of despair a moment ago – no wonder she was terrified of me! I turned to practicalities.

"Have you had any water or food?"

She shrugged dispiritedly, and pointed to where the bench met the wall behind me. In the fading light, I saw an empty half-liter plastic bottle and a crumpled white paper bag.

"Yesterday, *peut-être*. The day before..."

She had been without water for at least twenty-four hours. How long could a human survive without liquids? I suspected not more than two or three days. No wonder she seemed disoriented. How long would it be before I started to lose my grip too? I had eaten nothing since breakfast and drunk nothing since those two coffees in the park. Surely Hansen wouldn't leave us to die of thirst. Or would he? I still understood nothing about him or his intentions. No use speculating; my priority was Chantal.

"Are you injured? You are able to walk, yes?" I stretched out a tentative hand. She pulled abruptly away from me. Her change of expression shocked me: lips in a rictus grin, baring her teeth in what looked more like agony than a smile. Her shoulders jerked up and down. Was she laughing or crying? I was wary of touching her, even though my instinct was to hold her tight to stop her shaking. I waited until the spasm passed, and she could speak.

"He hurt me! Again and again! Up there!" She cast her eyes up in the direction of the above-ground rooms of the castle. "Then he left me down here with the other. That was worse! I begged him to take me back up there. I begged him—" She was becoming hysterical again, throwing her head from side to side, her voice now a shriek.

"Shhh, shhh, everything's alright, he won't hurt you again. I'm here to protect you ..." Foolish empty promises, but all I could think of to calm her. They didn't work.

"No! You don't understand! The other! It's my turn now—and yours!"

"What other? Who is the other?" But she was too far gone to answer me. All I could do was murmur meaningless phrases, while looking pointlessly around the cell for clues as to what she meant. There were no signs suggesting another occupant. Other than the blanket she clung to and the debris of her last "meal," the only unattached object was a plastic bucket in the corner – the toilet, by its stench. The bare stone walls rose up a dozen feet to a ceiling of rough planking. Two ominous iron rings were fixed near the roof's center. I pictured chains, and a prisoner hanging from them.

After a few minutes, Chantal's shaking slowed and she slumped forward. I squatted down in front of the bench to look into her face. Her eyes were open but her gaze was unfocused. I recognized that look from my own childhood horrors. She had retreated into a fugue state, the "safe" zone where the echoes of abuse could not reach her. Tears spilled from my eyes, this time, not in self-pity, but in empathy for Chantal. I could ascribe this unaccustomed urge to embrace and protect the poor girl as the late blossoming of maternal instinct. More reasonably, I was just identifying with her: she was the child victim I had once been.

From some deep-buried cache of memories I recalled a night spent shut in a smelly farm shed with my half-brother Shane. Glastonbury, was it? Or the Isle of Wight? My father telling us to enjoy our "camping adventure," as he and Mum ran off snickering to cadge drugs from the roadies backstage at the festival. Shane sang to me as we huddled under a pile of empty potato sacks, too scared to sleep. I think that was the beginning of my fear of rodents. I pushed the memory away; I could serve Chantal and myself better by concentrating on the present.

Chantal had been traumatized over a period of weeks, perhaps ever since she left Le Bec back in April. Hansen was obviously the main perpetrator. He had "hurt" her. Did that mean rape? Torture? As far as I could see in the dim light, she bore no physical wounds. She seemed more anxious about the recent experience with "the other" here in the cell. When she could speak again, I would try to gently urge the history out of her.

The oblong of sky visible through the high opening was only a shade lighter now than the surrounding stone. She allowed me to lay her down on the bench, where she instinctively curved into a ball against the wall, leaving me room to stretch out alongside her, and try to rest. But first, I steeled myself to use the malodorous bucket in the corner.

***

Amazingly, I managed some sleep, but in short bursts troubled by vague dreams of imprisonment, which blended into depressing reality each time I woke. I would hold my breath to listen for Chantal's breathing and stretch out a hand to feel her feverish forehead. In spite of her burning skin, she seemed to be sleeping quietly, the best thing for her. At one point, I twitched the blanket away from her body; I needed its warmth now more than her. I wore a sleeveless cotton dress while I could feel rather than see that she had on a long-sleeved sweater and pants. Clothes suitable for the brisk April day when she had left her home? Before the light failed I had noticed that her feet were bare and filthy, toenails yellowed and cracked.

During these periods of wakefulness, my brain worried uselessly at the possibilities of escape, like a hamster on a wheel. My eyes roamed the darkness until they ached – there was no moon after all, or it had set early. I closed them and tried to imagine myself elsewhere, at home, in bed, anywhere but here. For one blissful instant I imagined myself in Dykstra's arms, the feel of his hand on my waist, his lips on my throat, his smell …. but the illusion burst like a soap bubble, leaving me aching and empty. Where was he now? I was too exhausted to work out the time difference or remember his itinerary. Was he thinking of me? If I concentrated all my pathetic remnants of mental energy, could I pull his thoughts towards me? Could I make him hurry to France, discover my trail, and rescue me like a prince in a fairy story? Or maybe Pierre would piece together what we had discovered so far, call the police and …. Stupid me. Pierre and I had parted on poor terms. He owed no duty to a random American with an over-active imagination. He had his own demons to deal with. The only prince in this fable was me: if we were to be rescued, I needed a plan. The hamster wheel started spinning again.

Greyness began to penetrate the cell. I estimated it was about five a.m. although I could not make out the numbers on my watch. I eased away from Chantal's body, and stood up, stretching to relieve the ache from lying on a hard surface. I felt my way to the end of the bench where it butted up against the wall, and carefully lifted the plastic water bottle close to my eyes. Perhaps a couple of teaspoons of water remained in the bottom. I would get Chantal to drink that when she woke. My own throat was parched and swallowing was painful, and my head throbbed. I shuddered remembering news stories I'd read of victims trapped by earthquakes or landslides, force to drink their own urine.

I continued to edge my way around the walls, trying to learn as much as I could about our prison as the light slowly strengthened. The stones were uneven in size, as wide as a foot in some places, but with smaller, fist-sized rocks fitted in-between. They were cool and dry to the touch, except directly under the window opening, where I detected a clammy dampness. I guessed that recent rain had blown through and run down the wall.

Chantal stirred, and I crouched down beside the bench so as not to loom over her when she opened her eyes.

"*Qui êtes-vous?*" Her voice was still raspy, but her tone was calmer than the night before. Sleep had evidently done her troubled mind some good. I introduced myself again, and she nodded as if she remembered. I fetched the water and encouraged her to drain the last drops, which she did with a weary obedience. I wanted to find out what had happened to her since she left Le Bec in April, but hesitated to launch into questions. Instead, I rambled on about how Sam had spoken to Madame Albert, but he had not understood exactly what she said. I started to describe how Father Joseph, the curé, had revealed her desire to work with children, when she interrupted me.

"What's he like, my father?"

"He's tall, slim, with white curly hair—"

"No. His character, what is his character?"

"He is a good man, very kind and gentle, intelligent. He has devoted his life to helping people resolve conflict. He has been sad since his wife died last year. They were a wonderful couple."

Chantal brought her chin up and scowled. Perhaps that was insensitive of me. After all Sam and her mother had been a couple once.

"My mother told me that he abandoned us."

"I don't think that's true," I responded hesitantly. "Sam said your mother didn't like New York and returned with you to Limoges when you were a baby. He sent money, tried to stay in contact, but ...." I didn't want to argue the point with her. From her perspective, she had been abandoned. I doubted that Claire told her daughter that she returned Sam's letters unopened.

She shrugged, and turned her face away.

"It doesn't matter now."

I didn't want the silence to grow between us. I scrambled to keep the conversation going.

"And your mother? What was she like?"

Chantal pondered the question.

"She was beautiful ....." I thought she was going to elaborate, but then she just repeated, "*Belle*," in a hard tone that cut off further inquiry.

"Do you remember your father coming to see you when you were a child?"

Again, the chin came up.

"No. He never came."

I changed the subject.

"Tell me how you came to be here."

She stared, not at me, but through me. Silence stretched between us, and I began to fear she had retreated again into oblivion when she finally spoke.

"He said I was perfect. Perfect for the position, he said. The children would arrive soon, from all over Europe. A sanctuary, and I would be like a mother to them. A good mother, not like ... These children were abused, he said."

Several seconds passed before she resumed in a harsher voice.

"No children. He lied, except he did want me to play mother – to him!" She choked on the memory, and buried her face in her hands. I leaned closer to make out what she was saying.

"Sick, sick, perverted! He made me do things! Like a mother does for a baby! I didn't want to ... then he hurt me, made me do them. Said I wasn't doing it right, I was a bad mother, and he ... It was terrible. It didn't matter what I said or did, he found a reason to punish me. Eventually, he threw me in here with ……"

"The other?" I supplied. She shuddered still hiding behind her hands, and nodded.

"Chantal, who is the other?"

Just then a beam of morning sunlight penetrated our cell. I watched, mesmerized by the barred patch of brightness as it spread across the wall opposite the high opening. An omen? A visitation from a friendly spirit? I had almost forgotten my question when Chantal responded, lifting her face towards the light.

"A dead woman. He left me with a dead woman. I think I went mad. I don't remember much after that."

"Do you know how long you've been in here?"

She shrugged.

"Weeks. He took the body away, I don't know when. Sometimes he brings food, an empty bucket. He's going to kill us too, you know." She added this last comment in a dry, matter-of-fact voice. Perhaps, after what she had suffered, death seemed a welcome release.

"No, there has to be a way to get out. People will come looking for us." I tried to mask the tremor that undermined the confidence of my words. Chantal merely looked at me wearily, then turned her face upwards again to the shaft of sunlight, as if to drink it in before the sun rose higher and robbed us of its balm.

Chapter 16

France - Saturday

Time advanced at a glacial pace. I sat tense and still, as the morning hours crawled by, straining to hear the sound of approaching steps, but the exterior silence was unbroken, even by birdsong or the rush of wind through tree branches. At one point, I climbed onto the bench and stood on tip-toe to see if I could make out anything through the barred opening other than sky. A few blades of grass showing outside the bars confirmed that the cell was underground, with the bottom ledge of the opening level with the terrain. I gained no other clue about our surroundings, except that the sun's path showed our orientation was eastwards in the direction of the boundary road I had explored -- could it be? -- only two days before.

Was Hansen ever coming to feed us? To rape and kill us? As long as he came. I had formed the shell of a plan: as soon as he entered the cell, I would hurl the bucket of excrement at him, then grab Chantal's hand, drag her out and bolt the door. I rehearsed the moves in my head, and even paced them out nervously between the narrow confines of our dungeon's walls: over to the bucket, back behind the door, fling the bucket, grab Chantal, out the door, slide the bolt .... Over to the bucket ....

I didn't bother involving Chantal in this scheme. She had raised herself only enough to sit slumped against the wall, eyes open but unfocused. She moaned a couple of times, and I interrupted my rehearsal to rush to her side with soothing words that seemed not to connect. Her forehead was burning up again, and I feared that if someone didn't come soon it would be too late.

Sometime late morning, the sun stopped drilling directly into the cell, but the heat was still rising, and with it, the smell. What I had registered the night before as dank and musty was now decidedly rank and fecal. I concentrated on breathing through my mouth and turned my face up towards the oblong of sky visible through the opening. It did little good. I was sleep-deprived, but frightened that if I moved Chantal aside to stretch out on the bench again, I would doze off and miss the approaching steps that were our only hope.

The after-effects of the drug Hansen had administered were still in my bloodstream, making my head pound and driving spasmodic shivers through my body. My pacing became manic, and my thoughts repetitive. Random images penetrated my stupor like low-flying aircraft zooming through mist. Food: was I hungry? Not really, but I kept picturing the gourmet meal Jean Paul had served us at his subterranean restaurant. I stretched out an imaginary fork to spear a morsel of *foie gras mi-cuit,* but was nauseated as the phantom aroma of seared goose liver morphed into the stench of the slops bucket. I began to imagine faces in the shadowy corners of the oubliette. I struggled to name them but only Pierre's face was clear. He looked concerned. Was he worried for me, or for that First Nations girl who killed herself? Me! Me! I wanted it to be me! But Dykstra was my lover, not Pierre. Where was Dykstra's face? I couldn't find it. I knew his name but not his face. Panicked now, I fixated on cataloging all the faces I *could* remember: Gerardo, Heather, Sam, *Madame la patronne* at the hotel. Unbidden, my father's face loomed towards me: lank hair, spindly goatee and pinhole pupils. I fought for a different mental image, achieving only a picture of Hansen. Hansen and my father: what did they have in common, besides pasty complexions and thinning hair? The desire to hurt and a grandiose idea of themselves, the hallmarks of a sociopath. The enduring lesson I learned from my father was to put as much distance between me and him as I could. Now, my only hope lay in enticing a similar monster within arm's reach.

I was losing it, stuck in a maze, teetering between images of my father and Hansen, fighting to push back the full-blown anxiety attack that prowled around me like a wolf. I had to regain control for both our sakes. I gripped my upper arms fiercely, digging finger nails into flesh to shock myself to my senses, then took a deep breath through my nose. That did it. The stench brought me shuddering and choking back to reality.

Smell, that most evocative of senses. I sat down carefully on the edge of the bench, breathing deliberately through my mouth and trying to focus on another sense memory struggling to the surface of my brain. A bad smell, darkness, Pierre's concerned face. Yes! The body in Chantal's car!

"Chantal, listen to me. Where is your car? Did you drive it here? Chantal?"

Reluctantly, she dragged her eyes towards my face.

"My car?"

"Yes. Where did you leave it?"

She closed her eyes, and I thought she had drifted off again, but she was merely trying to pull her thoughts together.

"He drove it here. He made me wear a hood so I couldn't see where we were going. In case I refused the position, he said. The location is secret, you know." She looked at me seriously for a moment, then grinned. It was a horrible sight, a sniggering skull, a Halloween horror, and I had to force myself to keep my eyes engaged with hers. *"C'est drôle, n'est-ce pas?* How could he ever let me drive away if I refused the job? I didn't think of that!"

She turned her face back to the wall, smile fading away. I spoke more to myself than her.

"He used your car to take ... er ... the other," -- Damn it, I wouldn't adopt her macabre phrasing – "the dead woman who was here back to Le Bec. He hid the car and the body in the barn. Was she the first, or were there others? Is he a serial killer?" I added these questions in no more than a whisper, although Chantal was already drifting away into her own world.

Perhaps, when Hansen was at Le Bec, he took the opportunity to explore Chantal's home, and remove any clues to her whereabouts, as well as her laptop and personal papers. When I had gone through the rooms with Pierre on the day of my arrival in France, they seemed sanitized, denuded of the usual traces of day-to-day life, except for the contents of the refrigerator and the abandoned laundry. Perhaps Hansen's cleaning efforts had been interrupted. Of course! The stranger who pushed past Sam when he visited in April! I knew now that Hansen was a master of disguises. Sam had described only long dark hair in a ponytail, a fleeting impression before the intruder disappeared.

***

The lightning flash and crash of thunder were almost simultaneous. I jumped up, heart banging against my ribs. I had been dozing, in spite of my best intentions, sitting on the dirt floor, back against the rough stones. Chantal stirred but did not get up. She was curled into her habitual fetal position, face towards the wall, knees drawn up, face pillowed on hands.

Another flash and crash, then the rain started. Fat drops fell onto the stone sill at the lower edge of the opening. I positioned myself under it, head angled back in the hope that the storm would blow some of that moisture my way. Within a minute, individual drops became sheets of water pounding down and bouncing off the ledge. The stone could not absorb the volume of rain and gradually it started to spill over. I opened my mouth wide and stuck out my tongue as far as it would stretch. The gritty liquid tasted like salvation; the feel of water on my face was a benediction. Although I was reluctant to step away, I had to share this with Chantal.

"Wake up! The rain's coming in!" I held her under her arms and helped her to a seated position. She looked at me resentfully. Another lightning strike strobed through the cell, and Chantal turned to look up at the opening. She must have seen the light glistening on the rivulets now streaming over the sill, and realized what I meant because she allowed me to assist her over to the wall. I pinned her upright with an outstretched arm across her body. There we stood, like baby birds in the nest, cheeks pressed against the stones, faces turned upwards, and mouths gaping, oblivious to anything but the chance to capture every drop we could.

The time between the lightning flash and following boom of thunder lengthened as the storm moved away, but the rain continued to fall undiminished in intensity for several more minutes. I looked down at Chantal whose face was a scant eighteen inches from mine. Her closed eyelids were stretched thin, blue-ish and vulnerable. The rain had washed her hair back from her up-tilted forehead. For the first time, I saw an echo of her mother's beauty in that pale gleaming expanse, and in the high cheekbones hollowed out by hunger. What was she like really? What was her relationship with her mother, the mother who kept her unnaturally close right up to her death? Love and hate, I suspected; each blaming the other for their mutual dependency. But what did I know? I was guessing about a Chantal that may have existed months ago; *this* Chantal was abused, starved, near death. It might be that *in extremis* we reveal our true underlying character. Or, equally possible, we are reduced to an animal instinct for survival, stripped of social conditioning, just naked needs and Pavlovian responses. The truth: I didn't know her at all. I had come in search of -- and now bore the responsibility for -- an enigma.

My eyes traveled up from Chantal's face, across the window where the sky was now clearing, up to the dark angle above, between wall and beamed ceiling. Craning backwards, I noticed an oddly symmetrical shape, like a matte black golfball pressed into the space between the stones at the very top of the wall. Matte except for a glistening eye turned down towards the cell. A camera.

I cursed myself in a rush of impotent fury. Of course, a techie like Hansen would fit up the dungeon with surveillance. How stupid of me not to suspect that our every move – and worse, our every word – had been spied on. Then my anger turned again to Hansen. I imagined him gloating as I squatted over the disgusting latrine bucket, and laughing as I paced out my infantile escape plan. His perversions ran well beyond Oedipal play-acting with Chantal. He took pleasure in watching us being tortured by hunger and thirst. And we weren't the first. The woman in the car: she had died here, and he had watched it all, then watched Chantal as she went crazy in the company of the corpse. Next was Chantal, then me. The only reason he had barely sustained Chantal in life with scraps of food and water was to give him time to secure another victim in this gruesome series before she died.

The rain stopped. Intermittent drips still fell from the window sill, but I no longer arched my neck to catch them. Despair displaced anger. He would never come, not while we were both alive anyway. I felt Chantal sag against my arm, and considered whether to point out the camera to her. Wasn't it better to leave her in ignorance, to let her drift towards death now I concluded there was no hope of reprieve?

Knowledge is power. Miss Mumford's cut-glass accent sounded a hand's breadth from my ear. My foster parent, mentor and savior was a decade underground in a South London cemetery, but still her voice resonated in my head. *Ignorance; the root and stem of all evil.* Another favorite Mumford quote. I failed to see its relevance to the present situation but could not resist its mandate.

"Chantal," I whispered. "Look up there." She slowly opened her eyes and followed the direction I indicated with a tilt of my head. "Shhh. It's a camera. It's been recording our movements and, I think, our voices." The only positive thing I could grab onto was that, pressed hard against the wall under the opening, the camera angle could not cover us here.

"He's been watching us. Before I came, he watched you, and before you, the other woman. He's not going to come until we're dead."

She looked at me steadily. I didn't know if she understood me, or I had just confirmed facts she had already worked out for herself.

"*Donc, il faut mourir.*" Her delivery was dead-pan without a trace of irony; her face expressionless. Had I misunderstood the barely audible French? Was she really saying it was necessary to die? Was she just going to give up? While I looked questioningly at her, she gently disengaged herself from my supporting arm and staggered over to the bench. She arranged herself with painful slowness, on her side with face to the wall, knees drawn up and cheek again pillowed on hands.

It was then I made a second discovery that chased any thought of Chantal's probable death-wish from my mind. As the arm that had pinioned her to the wall fell to my side, my hand brushed over a fist-sized rock. It moved ever so slightly! I slid down the wall until I was sitting on the floor, my eyes level with the loose stone. I was fairly confident that the camera could not see me as I was immediately below it, but I was careful. I jiggled the rock gently to and fro, and some crumbs of the surrounding mortar fell out. The exterior part was rounded and fit comfortably into my palm. I tried to gouge out more mortar with my finger nails, but they were too short and weak to make any progress. I needed a tool, something metal that I could dig with. I mentally inventoried the cell again: nothing. I looked down over my bedraggled body. The summery cotton dress hung limply, stained with muddy run-off; the fashionable strappy sandals for which I had paid an outrageous sum in Atlanta looked ridiculously flimsy. Then I had an inspiration: my dress had a narrow self-fabric belt that fastened with a buckle. I undid the belt and ran my finger along the prong of the fastener. As I remembered, it was steel, an inch long and pointed. I went to work.

It took half an hour. Forgetting about Chantal, hunger or thirst, I concentrated all my attention on worrying away at the mortar that held the rock in place. I was careful to disguise the scratching by moving around and occasionally moaning, as well as taking long pauses, but when the rock finally came free there was an audible scrape that brought my heart into my throat. I froze for several seconds before examining my newly-liberated weapon: a piece of flint, weighing about a pound; one side – the one that protruded from the wall – was rounded; the end previously buried in the wall was faceted, sharp irregular edges that had gripped the mortar like claws over the centuries. Although I had no idea whether I would ever have a chance to use it, the mere feel of this object in my hand gave me strength.

Guiltily, my thoughts returned to Chantal. Hiding the rock in the folds of my skirt, I approached and bent over her, trying unsuccessfully to read her profile.

"Chantal?" No response. I hung there for several seconds, and just as I was starting to straighten up, her left eye, the only one visible to me, opened and blinked once, slowly and deliberately. A signaling wink? I couldn't tell. I watched for another half-minute but the eye remained closed, the face blank.

Playing dead. It was the only ploy left to us. A ploy that – for Chantal at least – might translate too quickly into truth. Who knew if it would work? Whether Hansen would come to extract the bodies, if he believed both or one of us to be dead? I retreated to a place where I calculated my face would be in shadow and sat down with my legs stretched out in front, my skirt fanned out over the hand gripping the rock.

There was nothing to do now but wait.

Chapter 17

France – Saturday Evening

I squinted down at my watch: six o'clock. Without moving my head, I could make out the dark hump of Chantal's body showing above the bench. How long could I stay motionless? My legs were cramping and the urge to scratch an itch at the corner of my eye was almost intolerable. But as long as Chantal kept still, I would.

I couldn't keep my thoughts still though. They darted between optimism and despair. How likely was it that Hansen would come, and if he came, that I could overpower him with my small rock? There were about three hours of daylight left. Once it got dark, I could relax a little; the camera would not pick up my movements and I could stretch out, maybe even use the damn bucket and check on Chantal. However, I prayed he would come before dark; the thought of another night in this hole in the ground was difficult to contemplate. I refused to entertain the thought that I might remain here indefinitely.

Assessing the chances that my disappearance had been noted, and that external help was on the way, I was forced to the conclusion that they were not good. My parting from Pierre on Thursday evening was cool and we had made no plans to meet again, so I couldn't expect him to be searching for me. My absence from breakfast this morning at the hotel was hardly likely to provoke a manhunt, nor were the overdue parking fees amassing on the abandoned rental car in Brantôme. Our best hope lay with Dykstra and Sam who would arrive tomorrow afternoon expecting to find me in St. Barthélemy. Yesterday's e-mail about the plan to follow Schiffer/Hansen to the Children's Home had likely caught them as they were either preparing to travel or were *en route*. They would not be concerned about my failure to send a follow-up report when they expected to see me in person so soon. I swallowed a sigh that might be picked up by video surveillance. I doubted whether I could retain my grip on sanity until Sam and Dykstra put the pieces together and mounted a rescue, even if I was still living. Chantal would not survive that long.

Six forty-five. My dress was still damp, but the freshness that had blown into the cell with the afternoon storm was just a memory. The smell of human waste and unwashed bodies crept over me and combined with an ancient smell of compounded misery, of prisoners recent and long past who had faced death here. I was again on the brink of giving up hope. The trial of suppressing my groans of despair was beginning to exceed even the painful challenge of keeping my body still. I could stand this no longer.

Just as I registered that thought, I sensed a sudden but subtle change in the light, as if a cloud had passed over the face of the sun. The only source of light was the barred opening above me, but the sun had long ago passed over to the other side of the building, so it could not have been a cloud. Something or someone outside had cast a shadow into the cell. I held my breath and waited.

"Hello? Wake up! I have food and water here for you." The voice was wheedling and sing-song, the baby-talk of someone who didn't like children. Hansen had finally come to check on us, but he had not entered through the door; he must be outside bending down to call through the opening. Stupidly, I had not anticipated that. What to do now? Abandon the pretense of death and take the life-sustaining provisions Hansen was offering to pass down to us? Or continue the charade in the hope that he would be enticed to open the cell door to make a closer examination? My response (or non-response) would be on Chantal's behalf as well as my own: the water we had managed to swallow during the storm might be enough to keep me going, but was it enough for Chantal? Her life might depend on getting nourishment immediately. But then Hansen might be tricking us; he might have no water or food with him. The dilemma careened around my brain in a matter of seconds, while Hansen hovered somewhere above me. I could hear him shifting, perhaps to get a better view into the dungeon. I decided to leave it in Chantal's hands: if she spoke up, so be it. If she was already dead or unconscious, I would gamble on him coming into the cell for a closer look. Time passed. Chantal did not stir.

"OK, OK." Hansen's voice retreated. I couldn't tell if he was disappointed that we were not cravenly begging food and drink from him, or satisfied that he had already watched our death throes.

My body felt electric. The hand gripping the stone clenched and unclenched. Heart drumming in my chest, I risked a few long, deep breaths to steady myself, trying to calculate how long it might take Hansen to walk from the exterior back inside and down the passage to our dungeon. Maybe he would not come directly here, but retreat to whatever viewing room he used to monitor the transmissions from the golfball camera and resume his ghoulish surveillance? Tense minutes passed as I ran through the possibilities.

Yes! Steps in the corridor followed by the rasp of the bolt being withdrawn. With my chin resting on my chest and through slitted eyes, I could only see the bottom of the door as it opened, and Hansen's feet approaching. I didn't breathe. He stood over me for a moment then crouched down. I could feel his sour breath on my downturned face. This was my chance. I knew I had to act decisively, but self-doubt paralysed me. Then I saw his hand approached my throat. At the first brush of his fingers, I lashed out with my left hand, fingers crooked to claw at his eyes. He grabbed my wrist in both his hands, and I swung my right arm round in an old-fashioned haymaker that connected behind his ear with a dull thwack. For a second we were cemented in this pose, faces a bare foot apart. His pale eyes registered surprise, before they rolled up into his head and he toppled over onto his side, loosening his grip on my wrist. I pushed him off my legs, scrambled to my feet, and ran over to Chantal.

"Chantal! Quick! We have to leave before he wakes up!" Terror gripped my stomach. Was she dead? It seemed an age before she uncurled from the fetal position she had assumed hours before. I took a deep breath of relief.

"*Il est mort? Dis-moi, est-il mort?*"

"No, Chantal, he's just unconscious. See? His chest is rising and falling. We have to get out of here!"

Weakness was making her movements unbearably slow. I winced at my roughness but we had to hurry. I grabbed her under her arms and pulled her up to standing. She threatened to fold, her eyes fixed on Hansen's body on the floor. I virtually dragged her to the door. She twisted her head back as we ducked under the low lintel.

"He is dead, *n'est-ce pas?*"

Just then, Hansen grunted, more an expulsion of air than a human sound.

"He's coming round. Quick!" I bundled Chantal out into the passageway, where she slumped against the opposite wall. I didn't take time for a last look into the cell before pulling the door closed and shooting the bolt home with a reverberating clang.

Chantal slid down the wall into a sitting position. Her eyes were closed. I wanted more than anything to get out of this place, to be in the open air, above ground, but she looked incapable of moving, and I knew I could not carry her.

"Listen, I'm going to look for something to drink and eat. I'll bring it back to you, and then, when you feel stronger, we'll find a way out together, OK?"

She gave a tiny nod. I stood there a moment longer, listening for any noise from the cell, and debating whether it was right to leave her in this state, so close to our enemy.

There seemed no alternative. I checked the bolt was firmly in place, placed my hand on Chantal's shoulder for a moment, hoping to reassure her, then set off up the long corridor I had travelled down the evening before.

I recalled the bend, the steps up, and the closed door on the left. Hoping it led to the outside, I tried the handle. The door opened into a storeroom of sorts, long and narrow, lined with industrial shelving, clerestory windows at ceiling height but no other exit. At least I might find something useful in these piles of cardboard boxes. I started with those closest: cleaning supplies, paper products, lightbulbs. Hansen seemed to have stockpiled enough to last for years. I turned to the other wall. This was more hopeful: cans of vegetables, bags of rice and pasta, surely there was something here that didn't need a can opener or a stove. Ah, finally! Cases of Heineken beer and Coca-Cola in bottles. I spent desperate minutes trying to prize the cap off a Coke before giving up. Neither beverage was probably the best choice on an empty stomach, anyway. I continued the search, and was rewarded a few boxes further along: liter bottles of Evian water. I grabbed two. Now to find some food that was ready to eat. I almost laughed out loud: the very next box contained packets of my favorite gourmet almond cookies from Belgium, a treat I allowed myself at home to celebrate the resolution of a thorny case. With two packets tucked under my arm, I started back towards the door.

I became conscious of a deep growling noise, like thunder, but continuous. It was louder as I emerged into the corridor. Above this low steady note was a repeated tack-tack beat. My exhausted brain struggled to identify the noise. It was coming from above my head and was building to a crescendo. Suddenly, I recognized it – a helicopter! Forgetting my promise to return to Chantal, I turned away from the direction I had come. In an ungainly run, clutching the water and cookies to my chest, I passed the door to what I remembered as "the computer room" -- the room with white walls and multiple monitors where I woke up yesterday. The corridor ended in an archway into a high-ceilinged room. A massive stone fireplace reared to my right, tall narrow windows – glazed this time – illuminated sparse but elegant furniture: leather sofas and low glass-topped tables. The sleek modern furniture contrasted with unplastered walls and flagstone pavers. Another corridor branched off at the far side of the fireplace. Perhaps it led to Hansen's living quarters. I was momentarily distracted by the thought of a kitchen, a bathroom, running water in which to plunge my face. But then I spotted the big double oak doors across the room: a way out! I rushed towards them, and awkwardly, still balancing my booty from the storeroom, lifted the latch to pull one door open. Stepping out into brilliant late-day sunshine, I was almost blown backwards by the gust from the rotor blades of a helicopter touching down on the grass about a hundred feet away.

After so many hours of inaction in the dim silence of the cell, the noise and bright light was overwhelming. I stood swaying at the top of a short flight of worn stone steps down to a patch of unkempt gravel, taking great lungfuls of fresh, grass-scented air. I squinted as five figures, clad in black with protective vests, jumped down from the helicopter. The first three also wore helmets and carried sub-machine guns in the ready position across their chests. The group spread out and approached at a slow run, crouched a little in the now-diminishing blast from the rotors.

"*Mademoiselle McKinney! Comment ça va?*" I didn't at first recognize Inspector Parmentier, even though he was not one of the helmeted men. Shouted over the engine noise, his commonplace greeting, as if he had just encountered me in a local café, threw me further.

"In there ... Chantal Dubenoit. She was Hansen's prisoner." I gestured behind me, grasping for the words that would explain the situation he would find inside.

Parmentier didn't wait.

"You two, come with me! You, open the entrance for the others, and you," He pointed at the remaining *gendarme*, "Stay with her!" He pushed past me to the double doors.

"Wait! Take this." I thrust a bottle of water and a box of cookies at him. He reared back as if a madwoman had threatened him. "Chantal needs them!"

Reluctantly, the inspector took the proffered goods, and disappeared into the building. The crunch of footsteps on gravel receded, as another policeman headed for the line of trees to the east. The rotor blades came to a standstill, and in the resounding silence I turned to the man at my side. He looked surprisingly young, with peach-down cheeks and plump red lips, a boy playing soldier. His brows were drawn together, a frown to bolster an impression of fierceness to counteract his youth. Maybe he was peeved at having drawn the short straw and been left to guard a disheveled American while others had the more exciting job of exploring the interior. I gave him an uncertain smile, and he nodded curtly in response.

But his reticence could not drown the dawning realization that I was free, alive, unhurt, and had accomplished my mission! I had found Chantal and tomorrow she would be reunited with Sam. I closed my eyes, raised my face to the setting sun, and offered a silent prayer of thanks to whatever Greater Being, Life Force or Pure Chance had led to this outcome.

I unscrewed the Evian bottle and cautiously sipped, mindful that the greedy gulps I wanted to take would lead to an ugly rebellion in the stomach. I tore open the cookies and, leaving the package on the steps, nibbled on one as I walked out onto the grass. The young policeman continued to scowl, but didn't follow me. After the confines of the cell, it was pure joy to stretch my legs. I stopped about half way to the helicopter, and turned to look at the exterior of La Bastide for the first time. The central part – probably the castle keep in medieval days – rose up forty feet to uneven crenellations, where archers had once fired down on attackers. The stonework at the top was broken in several places; there were unglazed openings in deep embrasures. Lower down, however, the walls were better maintained and the windows wider. On each side of the keep, apron walls angled back.

These were lower, no more than twenty feet at their highest point where they joined the main building, then dwindling into ruins overgrown with creeper.

My guess was that a bird's eye view would reveal that this crumbling façade artfully hid modern renovations behind: the entrance hall I had passed through, the computer room, storeroom and passage down to the oubliette on one side, and more rooms on the other, along the corridor I had not taken time to explore. Maybe these accommodations were also disguised from above so that even a bird, or the all-seeing eye of Google Earth, would only make out ancient ruins. With his seemingly impenetrable perimeter wall, Hansen had made the castle into a recluse's ideal, a place to pursue his perverted pleasures without fear of discovery. At the same time, modern technology – that was after all Hansen's *métier* – enabled him to spy on others, both inside and outside the compound, and use the internet to manipulate them. I craned up to see if I could make out any high-tech paraphernalia, but if there was any, it was invisible from this angle.

The *gendarme*'s radio crackled into life, and I made my way back to the steps. He turned ostentatiously away to mutter into his shoulder, in imitation of a hundred TV cop shows, but there was no risk I could understand the garbled French police jargon being exchanged. Half a minute later the grumble of motor vehicle engines drew my eyes to the trees to the east. As I watched, a police patrol car emerged, followed by a white van that might be an ambulance. The vehicles lurched over a rutted overgrown path I had not noticed before, and drew up on the gravel in front of La Bastide. Two uniformed policemen jumped out of the car and jogged over to their colleague. Behind them, another figure, this one not in uniform, climbed out of the back seat: Pierre!

I was so happy to see him. I rushed forward to throw myself into his arms. At the last moment, some instinct checked me: hadn't I regretted breaching boundaries with Pierre before? Our eyes met; I saw a spark in his that I could not interpret before he swept me into a crushing bear hug. It felt wonderful.

"Are you OK? I've been so worried!"

Laughing, I reassured him that I was fine, all the finer for seeing him and being able to speak in English again. "My brain has completely run out of French!"

Just then, a commotion behind us signaled that the search party had emerged, Inspector Parmentier supporting Chantal on one side, another policeman on the other. Her eyes were slitted against the sunlight and I couldn't tell if she saw me when I called out her name. Two white-coated attendants from the van – it *was* an ambulance then – took over, and helped Chantal into the back.

"Wait! I'm coming with you!"

I hurried to the back of the van in time to have the doors slammed shut in my face. Parmentier pulled me out of the way by the arm. The ambulance started up and made a wide turn back towards the trees, leaving muddy tracks in grass still wet from the afternoon storm.

"But Chantal needs me! She's been imprisoned for God knows how long, she's been abused, starved! Her father's arriving tomorrow. I want to stay with her!"

I was speaking in English, turning from Parmentier to Pierre who came up to stand on my other side. Parmentier ignored me, talking over my head to direct his response to Pierre. I heard a distance in his tone that had not been there before he entered the building.

"Mademoiselle Dubenoit needs medical attention. She is being taken to the hospital in Montbrun." He named the midsized town between St. Barthélemy and Limoges. "Meanwhile I have questions for Mademoiselle McKinney. I require her to come with me to the *gendarmerie* for an interview." He refused to meet my eyes.

"But you can see she's exhausted! Surely the questions can wait until tomorrow."

"*Non, mon Père*," – the sarcasm in his use of the religious title was unmistakable, especially as Pierre was dressed unclerically in an open-necked shirt and jeans – "This cannot wait."

Parmentier swung around to face me, letting go of my upper arm, but still standing intimidatingly close. He spoke slowly and emphatically.

"There is a dead man in there." He jerked his head towards the double doors. "I would like to know who killed him and why. *Compris*?"

Dead? How could Hansen be dead? He was alive when we locked him in the oubliette. I didn't hit him that hard. Or had I? My legs felt like rubber, and I thought I was going to faint. If it weren't for Pierre holding me up, I would have fallen.

"No ... he was breathing, he made a sound! I didn't mean to—"

Pierre broke in, speaking fast and *sotto voce,* telling me what, as a lawyer, I should have known to do, if I wasn't in shock.

"Don't say anything else now."

Chapter 18

Saturday Evening

I sat in silence next to Pierre in the back of the police car, still clutching my water bottle. Inspector Parmentier was in the passenger seat, alternately texting and speaking to the *gendarme* who drove. We bounced along the rutted track and were quickly swallowed up amongst the trees. The path chicaned to left and right, then dead-ended at a metal structure, like a half-built barn. The side we approached was open. As we slid under the roof, I saw that the further side was mostly made up of an overhead garage door. The driver got out and busied himself with a computer console on a shelf at one side. The garage door rattled up to reveal a country lane. I understood then that what I had dismissed as an abandoned workshop during my reconnaissance earlier in the week was the very private entrance to Hansen's domain. At least one mystery was solved as we left the grounds of La Bastide.

The wave of relief that had carried me forward since breaking out of the cell abruptly ebbed when Parmentier announced Hansen's death. I felt numb, my brain unable to process the fact of his death, that I had killed him. How was that possible? I stared out the car window as we sped towards St. Barthélemy, seeing nothing.

Pierre tried to distract me by filling in the details of how we had come to be rescued. He had gone to find me at the hotel that morning, feeling bad about the cool way we had parted company on Thursday. Madame, the innkeeper's wife, told him I had not appeared at breakfast, and, in her annoyingly gossipy way, she explained that I had set off for Brantôme on Friday morning "pretending to be a tourist." She, however, astutely putting together my inquiries about La Bastide from the day before, smelled a mystery! She insisted on using her master key to confirm that my bed was unslept in before Pierre could get away.

He had no difficulty finding my little Peugeot rental car in the popular parking lot on the north end of Brantôme, a bright orange parking ticket conspicuously flagging the windshield. The car was unlocked, and, as he sat in the driver's seat puzzling over what to do next, he noticed my cell phone in the space between the two front seats.

"You really should have a password, Sarah," he said, smiling gently. Since I swapped my Blackberry for a Smartphone at the start of the year, I had been meaning to add a password lock, but the task had escaped me; I was not as technologically adept as I liked to think I was. "I finally worked out how to get into your sent messages" – he was no techie either – "and saw that you were planning to follow someone called Schiffer to where Chantal was supposed to be living. That's when I phoned *him*."

Pierre slid his eyes towards Parmentier's back. The inspector was concentrating on his phone, but Pierre dropped his voice.

"It took a while but I persuaded him we should check out La Bastide. When we couldn't find a way into the place, he called in reinforcements. It seemed to take a lot of time to organize. I wish we could have got there sooner, before ...."

I turned back to the window. Yes, perhaps if the police had arrived sooner, Hansen would have been arrested, not killed. But more probably, he would have protested his ignorance of Chantal's and my existence, and refused to let them search the place. After all, having a disguised entrance was hardly probable cause that a crime has been committed.

"Thank you, Pierre. If you hadn't persuaded Parmentier to take an interest, we'd still be trapped back there. I'm really grateful." I sighed and closed my eyes. I should have been planning for the interview ahead, how to describe everything that had happened since I had received Chantal's – no, Hansen's – e-mail yesterday, but I was just too tired.

***

The St. Barthélemy *gendarmerie* occupied the rear portion of the same 1930's building that housed the *mairie,* the town hall. But while the front façade was all art deco elegance, the police station was strictly utilitarian. We entered through a dark grey metal door, leaving the indigo velvet of the evening for a glaringly strip-lit area with a concrete floor and a counter at one end. The officer on duty greeted Parmentier who grunted in reply. A couple of elderly men in shabby clothes sat on metal seats bolted to the wall. They stared at the floor, showing no interest in our arrival. I was led past them and through a door at the left of the counter into an equally brightly-lit office furnished with ranks of desks at which a few men and women, some in uniform and some not, were working. They seemed as unimpressed by my entrance as the men waiting outside. Perhaps I had become invisible. Light-headed with fatigue, I imagined my body dissolving and floating apart in wisps of transparent mist.

Behind me, Parmentier and Pierre were arguing about something. I stopped to concentrate on their exchange, trying to shake off the sense of detachment that had overtaken me in the car. Parmentier was attempting to prevent Pierre from accompanying me further.

"She was perfectly able to answer my questions in French the other day. She doesn't need an interpreter." The inspector towered over Pierre, and outweighed him by about a hundred pounds, but Pierre held firm.

"She wasn't exhausted and in shock then. She's been through a terrible ordeal. You should postpone the examination until tomorrow, but if you insist on going forward, *I* insist on being present to translate your questions into English and her responses into French."

"This is just an informal interview, not an examination."

"So she has the right to refuse to speak to you?"

Pierre turned to me. I vaguely understood this was my cue. I spoke in English, addressing Parmentier. It was not an act. I had totally exhausted my French vocabulary.

"Please, let Pierre stay. I want to explain what happened, but I need his help with the French."

Exasperated, the inspector shrugged. He must be under quite a lot of pressure, a small town policeman with two suspicious corpses turning up in less than a week. He had been abrupt but polite when he questioned me at Le Bec; now he was downright surly. Perhaps my appearance at the scene of both discoveries explained his attitude, or he just didn't like Americans, or women in general.

"*Bien.* Follow me." He pushed on across the room but I didn't move.

"First, I need the bathroom .... *La toilette?*"

I thought for a moment he was going to refuse, his scowl was thunderous, but then he beckoned to one of the female police.

"Take her to the ....," he mumbled, waving his fingers dismissively.

I followed along a corridor to a door marked "*Dames.*" *Was the policewoman going to come in with me*? I thought in panic, but she smiled pleasantly and walked away.

I would never take flush toilets and running water for granted again. When I emerged five minutes later, I felt much more human, and I was ready to talk. My law school classmates and fellow associates at the New York law firm would have screamed in protest – "Insist on having a lawyer! Ask to call the U.S. Consulate! They can't keep you here!" – but I found myself thinking of Margaret Mumford, that fount of relevant quotations: "And the truth shall set you free!" I also heard an echo of my other good angel, Marta Cantor, describing the mediation process in her usual dramatic fashion: "Being *listened to*, being *heard*: it's the most empowering thing in the world!" Certainly, as a mediator – the listener – I had observed that to be the case. Now I was going to test the proposition from the other side.

I found my way back to the general office, and the same smiling policewoman escorted me to a room where Parmentier and Pierre were already installed on opposite sides of a conference table. A coffee pot, three mugs and – incongruously – a dry-looking fruit cake on a plate – perhaps the only food they could scrounge up at this hour? – sat in the center. Parmentier indicated a chair at the head of the table, and poured the coffee.

"Now, tell me everything that happened since yesterday morning."

I began with reading the response to my e-mail, which set up the meeting in the riverside park in Brantôme. I described Schiffer/Hansen, reporting as closely as I could remember what he had said and what I had said. I stopped every couple of sentences to allow Pierre to translate, using the pause to organize what I was going to say next. I kept it factual, not editorializing on how stupid I felt to have fallen into his trap. Parmentier took copious notes. From time to time, he looked as if he was going to interrupt with a question, but restrained himself, pursing his lips and frowning. Once, he held up his meaty hand to stop me, but it was only so that he could catch up with his scribbling. He poured another round of coffee – it was surprisingly good, although the fruit cake was indeed stale and I declined a second slice – and gestured for me to start again.

I described the oubliette and Chantal's miserable condition. Then I hesitated.

"Has someone spoken to Chantal? Has she said what happened to her before I arrived?" I was uncomfortable relating what she had said to me about Hansen's fetishes. It wasn't prudishness, but an ingrained reluctance to engage in hearsay. What if, out of misplaced shame or an exaggerated sense of privacy, she denied that part of the story?

"No. Mademoiselle Dubenoit is under sedation at present. I will speak to her tomorrow."

I made the decision to plunge forward, breaking into French only so that I could faithfully relay the words Chantal had used herself. Parmentier looked up sharply when I spoke about "the other" – the corpse in the cell – and the fact that Chantal's car was originally parked at La Bastide. I left him to draw the conclusion that Hansen must have used it to transport the woman's body to Le Bec.

I was glad to resume speaking English to describe the storm, the discovery of the camera, and the loose stone in the wall, and our plan to play dead to entice Hansen into the cell. Again, the inspector held up a palm to slow me down. We were approaching the critical part. I took a sip of cold coffee and listened to the scratching of pen on paper as Pierre translated.

"I am sure he was breathing when I locked him in the cell. He made a sound. I thought he was coming to, so I hurried Chantal out, and went to find water for her. That's when I heard the helicopter," I concluded.

Parmentier put down his pen, and sorted through his notes, stopping to read over a section here and there. I dreaded the next step. He was either going to take me back to the beginning and pick through every fact, asking for details, questioning my perceptions, or he was going to arrest me for murder. The need to get my story out had energized me, but now exhaustion overtook me again. My throat hurt and my eyes ached; I sagged in my seat.

"Zank you, Meess McKinney." Having exhausted his supply of English, the inspector switched back to French. "The technical team is searching La Bastide at this moment. I will alert them to look for video from the camera in the cell. The autopsy will take place early tomorrow. I will speak to you again after we have more information. At noon?"

I nodded. Anything to get out of here and back to my hotel room.

As soon as we were in the corridor, we could hear raised voices. They were coming from the waiting area on the other side of the general office. It sounded like the same argument that had taken place earlier that evening between Parmentier and Pierre, one wanting to come in, and the other trying to keep him out. The participants were different this time, although one voice was confusingly familiar.

"Dykstra!" I stumbled forward into the office, knocking against chairs, pushing past the surprised *gendarme* blocking the door to the outer area, and literally fell into his arms.

***

On the walk back to the hotel, Dykstra explained that when he landed at Heathrow that morning and found no follow-up to my e-mail about following a stranger to Chantal's new place of employment, he decided to skip his planned one-night layover in London and catch the next available flight to the Dordogne. His instinct that I was walking into some kind of trap was much more acute than mine had been. He had left a message for Sam who would follow on from Heathrow the next day as previously arranged. When he arrived at the hotel earlier that evening, Madame gave him an animated recap of Pierre's morning visit, together with lurid theories about what had become of me. He followed her directions to La Bastide, and found a police car stationed there on the lane. The *gendarme* refused to tell him anything, so he turned around and sped back to St. Barthélemy. It was nearly ten o'clock at night and Parmentier's "informal interview" was wrapping up by the time he located the *gendarmerie* and extracted a confirmation out of the desk officer that I was inside.

Thankfully, Monsieur was on duty in the hotel lobby when we arrived. Quietly discreet as his wife was brashly inquisitive, he confirmed Dykstra's reservation starting the next day, but regretted that there was no room available for tonight. It was the weekend and the summer season was beginning; the hotel was full. He nodded agreeably when I proposed that we could share, and wished us both a *"bonne fin de soirée"* without a trace of insinuation.

Dykstra took off his shoes and stretched out on the bed while I took a hot shower. I wrapped myself in a towel, and was combing through my wet hair as I stepped back into the bedroom to find Dykstra fast asleep, his hands clasped over his stomach. His snores were gentle rhythmic purrs that drew me to lie down beside him and stroke his head as if he were a dozing cat. He did not stir. I thought about waking him to get him to undress, but decided to let him sleep on; he had had a long day, too. I pulled the other side of duvet over me.

After all that had happened, I thought I would drift effortlessly into sleep, but instead my hamster-wheel brain began churning through recent and not-so-recent events. In the less than ten months since I had met the man sleeping by my side, I had been shot, burgled, kidnapped, tortured with a lighted cigarette and nearly thrown overboard into the nighttime sea. I could not directly ascribe my capture and imprisonment by Hansen to Dykstra's account, but I suspected my underlying motive in coming alone to France to search for Chantal in the first place had been to impress him.

And now I had killed a man. How did I feel about *that*? I heard the echo of my erstwhile therapist's voice. In the far-off days when I worked for the New York law firm and had group health insurance, I had seen her for the lifetime maximum-permitted ten sessions. It had been a game, really: she, probing my emotional scar tissue with increasing intensity as our hour wound to a close; me, resisting demurely, revealing only what I felt I could safely discuss without breaking down, with one eye on the clock, at once dreading and longing for the session to be over. No doubt the experience was exasperating for her, but it was my dime, and back then I felt I got my money's worth. I learned the breathing and meditation techniques that served me well during the random panic attacks that still ambushed me. I adopted her active listening routines in my mediation practice, and even parroted her questions about fundamental feelings to get past the adversarial positions assumed by parties and their lawyers.

So how *did* I feel?

On the one hand, I was glad Hansen was dead; he was an evil man. His death meant neither Chantal nor I would have to face him at trial, relive our experiences and risk them being discounted or disbelieved, and Hansen going free. I could justify his death as self-defense: I was in fear of my life, it was kill or be killed. I saved Chantal, who might not have survived much longer if I had not acted. And, after all, I had not *meant* to kill him. Even in my head, that excuse sounded whiney, like a child caught out in some minor infraction.

So *there* was the root of my sleeplessness: killing Hansen awoke in me the feelings I had spent my adult lifetime suppressing. Killing Hansen took me back to the dark, enclosed place where bad things happened, the sour smell of a drinker's breath, the taste of blood in my mouth, and the whispered threats in my ear. In that moment when the stone made contact with his skull, I had *wanted* to kill him.

Chapter 19

Sunday

The church bell penetrated my turbulent sleep. The sense of having lost something precious, the trailing end of a bad dream, clung to me. I started counting the chimes to work my way to full consciousness. At thirteen I realized today was Sunday, and the bell was not marking the hour but calling people to mass. As I hitched myself up against the pillows, I felt tears on my cheeks and wiped them away with the sheet.

Dykstra had cracked the shutter to let in some light, and was sitting on the far edge of the bed, tapping away at his laptop. He turned to smile at me, and the last melancholy traces of the dream vanished. We kissed gently, hands cupping each other's faces. I had missed this; the way we started slow with soft fingertip brushes, resisting the heat building between us until our bodies could not be denied union any longer.

The chimes were calling the faithful to the next mass when we finally untangled our limbs. Dykstra sat up slowly and began to log out of the laptop he had abandoned to make love with me.

"What are you working on?" I indicated the computer.

"Research. One of Europ News' stringers in Sweden has sent me some deep background on Torkil Hansen, the owner of La Bastide." Dykstra read from the screen. "Seems he was a technology entrepreneur in the first internet boom. Still in his teens when he developed face recognition software that's now used world-wide for crowd control and security screenings, and only twenty-four when he sold his company to a U.K. technology giant called Tiber for a record-breaking sum in May, 2002. After the sale, he dropped completely out of sight. This journalist finally tracked him down to 'a remote area of rural France,' where he lives 'in a medieval fortress made impregnable by modern technology.' He refused to be interviewed for the story, and the writer speculates that it was the death of his mother in late 2002 that led this 'young genius to adopt a reclusive lifestyle.' Hmm, he seems to have had a troubled childhood."

I tensed. I had never told Dykstra the details of my early life, only that it was not happy, and that I had been glad to escape the U.K. to take up a scholarship at an American college. Hansen's background was an interesting coincidence, nothing more, and I deliberately relaxed my jaw.

"How 'troubled'?" I asked.

"He was the only child of a single mother, but it's not that. It's that his mother was apparently mentally ill for long periods during Hansen's teen years, and right up until she died. The death was ruled accidental, a drug overdose, but there were rumors."

"Of suicide?"

"That or …." Dykstra leaned into the screen, his profile illuminated. "Hansen and his mother lived a very isolated life in northern Sweden, especially after he dropped out of school and developed the face recognition software. No other family, no friends – for either of them, it seems. They were reported to be very close, but that's what people always say. Hansen never gave interviews."

"What kind of mental illness did his mother suffer from?" I got out of bed and started rooting in my suitcase for something to wear.

"Don't know. The medical records are confidential. My guy deduced mental illness from the fact that she was in a psychiatric facility on four separate occasions between 1994 and 2002. In 1994, he was only fifteen. Huge burden for a young kid." Dykstra shut the laptop.

A flash of anger pushed me upright.

"So we're supposed to feel sorry for him now? How do we know he didn't drive her into depression, or even if she was ill at all? He might have signed her into those places against her will." I felt my cheeks on fire.

"Sarah! What's the matter? Why are you so upset? I'm not excusing him, or what he did to you and Chantal. I guess I'm trying to understand why he's such a monster."

I realized that I was over-reacting. I needed to get a grip; my emotional barometer had been off-kilter from the moment I set foot in France, and the last forty-eight hours had pushed me to the edge. Even though I had escaped La Bastide, I still had hurdles to face, not least a possible charge of murder. I should not let my insecurities undermine Dykstra's faith in me.

"I'm sorry. I didn't sleep well and I'm still jumpy from everything that happened. Forget it. I'm so hungry! Why don't you get in the shower and then we'll go down to breakfast. What time does Sam's flight get in?"

I thought I had successfully distracted him from my outburst. While he showered, I finished dressing, then exchanged places with him in the tiny bathroom to brush my hair and put on some minimal make-up to disguise the shadows under my eyes.

I spoke through the sliding door.

"I'd like to get my car back from Brantôme. Can you drive me? Then we could go check in on Chantal at the hospital in Montbrun before I have to go back to the police station at noon."

***

Another sunny day. The terrace was crowded with breakfasting guests. Even so, Madame made a beeline to our table, waving off a request for more coffee from some guests browsing the buffet. Clearly she felt her role in directing

Pierre, and then Dykstra, to La Bastide entitled her to a full account of my incarceration and rescue. I left the talking to Dykstra, who skillfully persuaded her that, while he *could* reveal more at a later date and in a more private setting, the matter was under active investigation and all witnesses had been sworn to maintain confidentiality.

Meanwhile I piled my plate with translucent shavings of pale pink ham, two hard boiled eggs, a plump croissant and a dollop of homemade apricot jam, then went back to the buffet for a bowl of creamy yoghurt sweetened with local honey. This was my first meal in two days and I intended to enjoy it.

A few minutes later, I looked up to find Dykstra surveying me reflectively.

"He likes you, you know. Pierre."

"What? No! Well, not like that. He's a priest."

"He's also a man. And didn't you say he was 're-examining his vocation'?" Dykstra's crooked fingers made those little "quote" signs in the air that I hate. I flashed back to the night before. I had been so elated to see Dykstra, and in such a hurry to get out of the police station, that I had rushed through the introductions. Now I remembered there had been a moment's hesitation – Dykstra looking doubtfully at Pierre's extended hand – before they shook.

I tried for a light, teasing tone, but it came out sounding tinny.

"Why, *Monsieur* Dykstra, I do believe you're jealous!"

"I just wish I hadn't let you come to France on your own."

Let me! I bit down on the rage that swept over me. The spoonful of yoghurt on my tongue turned bitter, and I swallowed it with difficulty. I kept my voice level and my eyes on my plate, but I knew my face was burning again.

"Pierre has been a tremendous help in finding Chantal and in getting us both out of that place. I'm grateful to him. *You* should be grateful to him too."

I raised my eyes. To my astonishment, Dykstra's eyes were full of tears.

"It's just that I was so worried. I want to protect you, but it seems I always lead you into danger."

Instinctively, I stretched my hand across the table to his. I couldn't stay mad at him. His flashes of arrogance were always balanced by revelations of vulnerability.

"This time, it wasn't your fault. I was an idiot, but in the end, I found Chantal for Sam, which is what I set out to do." *And now I face a possible murder charge.* "I think you can still protect me, by doing what you do best. Go for the story; find out about Hansen, what he's done and why he's done it. Parmentier wants a quick resolution, but this may go deeper – and even darker – than it seems."

***

Dykstra turned in his rental car at the Brantôme agency after we had picked up my vehicle and paid the hefty fine at the *Bureau de Stationnement*. Sam would be arriving this afternoon and it made no sense to have three rental cars. The bright orange parking ticket had proved an effective defense against car thieves, because, not only had Hansen left the car unlocked, but the keys were still in the ignition. I wondered if he had relied on some opportunist stealing the vehicle and so frustrating any search for me. However, he had snatched up my bag containing my wallet, so Dykstra needed to cover my debt. I hoped I'd be able to pick up my belongings at the *gendarmerie* later; the search of La Bastide should be completed by now.

Neither of us referred again to the earlier spat, but its shadow hung over us as we drove north to the hospital at Montbrun. Perhaps I should find Dykstra's suspicion of Pierre flattering. If I were more secure about my own feelings I would, but instead, his possessiveness felt like just another reason not to get too emotionally involved with him. That remark about regretting "letting me" come to France alone still rankled, but maybe I had dismissed Dykstra's assessment of Pierre's feelings for me too cavalierly. Pierre had met me at a particularly vulnerable point in his life. Had I been guilty of using him, not only in the search for Chantal, but again last night, to run interference with the police and protect me from arrest? Did Pierre think I was leading him on? Working out my own feelings was difficult enough; fathoming everyone else's expectations was altogether too demanding.

The hospital was a modern building. Housed in a glass atrium, the main reception area reminded me of a hotel. Luxuriant tropical plants flanked seating areas; there was even a water feature tinkling away. The immaculately made-up receptionist was garbed in a pale pink uniform, half-way between nurse and flight attendant.

"Chantal Dubenoit is on the third floor, section B, room 319."

As we turned away to find the elevators, she called us back.

"But it says here, no visitors."

"Why? Is she very ill?" I had assumed that once Chantal was in medical hands, the worst was over, and she would recover quickly from the privations of the last weeks.

The receptionist gave a typical Gallic shrug, lips pouffed out.

"I don't know. Better to ask at the nurses' station on the third floor. The elevators are over there."

The elevator doors opened at the third floor to a more recognizable hospital environment. Brightly lit corridors labeled A and B led off to right and left. Ahead, the nurses' station bristled with computer screens, crash carts and wheelchairs.

I approached one of the personnel behind the desk.

"Can you tell me, how is Chantal Dubenoit? She's in room 319."

After a few clacks on the keyboard, and barely glancing up at me, the nurse replied.

"She passed a comfortable night. Two units of IV hydration. She's awake now."

"Can I see her, just for a minute? Her father is arriving today from America. She hasn't seen him for many years, and I wanted to prepare her—"

"No visitors!"

"Why? If she's awake and rested—"

"She is allowed no visitors." The nurse pointed at the screen in front of her, as if the words appearing there were Holy Writ.

"But on whose orders? Surely, it wouldn't hurt to let me see her just briefly?"

I was beginning to hate those typical Gallic shrugs. Sometimes they meant "I don't know," and sometimes, as here, they imparted the additional sense of "I couldn't give a damn." I remained at the counter, smiling fixedly at her. After a few moments, she relented.

"You could speak to the doctor. She's with a patient right now, but will be available in a few minutes. The waiting area is round there." She pointed up corridor B. "First door on the left."

Dykstra led the way, but the moment we were out of sight of the nurses' station, he put a finger to his lips and jerked his head towards the further end of the corridor. There sat a *gendarme*, back against the wall, chin on chest. We crept on past the door marked *"Salle d'Attente."* The numbering on the other doors confirmed my conclusion that the policeman was guarding room 319, Chantal's room. His head jerked up as we reached him, but he was too slow to stop Dykstra opening the door and entering, with me close behind.

Chantal was propped up against pillows, wearing a green hospital gown that reflected a sickly light onto her pale face. Her hair had been washed and was held back from her face with a narrow hair band. From the grease-darkened rat's nest she wore in the cell, it had resumed the mid-brown color of the photo with Paulette's daughter. Her eyes were ringed with shadow. When she saw me, they flew open for a split second, then half-closed, expressionless.

Dykstra had entered ahead of me and stood to my right, his body masking the figure sitting by Chantal's bedside. Inspector Parmentier now rose and bore down on us, pointing an angry finger.

"What are you doing here?"

Suddenly the small room was filled with people and noise: Parmentier continuing his harangue, Dykstra lifting his palms in an attempt to explain and placate, and the corridor guard who followed us in, whining excuses. A female voice cut through the racket and we turned as one to the doorway where an imposing white-coated figure stood, with a stethoscope – the universal badge of medical authority – hanging around her neck.

"Out, all of you! Now! Mademoiselle Dubenoit needs rest."

Even the husky inspector seemed to shrink as he obediently slunk out of the room. I was the last to leave. I looked at Chantal again. She had an inscrutable Mona Lisa half-smile on her face; as I turned to follow the others, she gave me the tiniest of nods.

The doctor introduced herself as Sylvia Madjeska, but seemed uninterested in our identities, or in Parmentier's explanation that he was here to conduct a criminal investigation. She spoke over his protest.

"Although she is recovering well physically, the extent of the mental trauma remains to be determined. I have called in a psychiatrist who specializes in such cases for an assessment. He should be here later today. No interrogation until after that."

"Her father is arriving today. Can he see her?"

The doctor looked down her aristocratic nose at me.

"There is no father listed in her records, and her mother is dead. I will not allow her to be harassed by strangers—" here, she glowered again at Parmentier, "—until after the psychiatric assessment. Come back tomorrow." With that she swept away down the corridor.

"Let's talk," Parmentier grunted, his hand under my elbow. He steered me back to the waiting room where he gave some whispered instructions to the *gendarme*, who headed off for the elevators, then he ushered Dykstra and me inside. The room was bland, beige on beige, at odds with the hotel-lobby-style three floors below. Parmentier wrangled three hard plastic chairs into a triangle and we sat down.

"*Bien*, Meess McKinney, tell me. How many times did you hit Torkil Hansen?"

"Once! Just once! Didn't Chantal tell you—"

"Mademoiselle Dubenoit told me that she remembers nothing, nothing at all, from the time she was taken to La Bastide until she was rescued by the police."

I sat still, taking this in and working out the implications.

"You have the medical report." I made it a statement, not a question, but Parmentier nodded slowly twice.

"And it shows …?" Dykstra chimed in. Parmentier glanced at him but spoke to me. He seemed less churlish today. I noted he was wearing the same clothes as yesterday and was in need of a shave. He must have been up all night.

"Torkil Hansen died from multiple blows to the head. It cannot be determined which was the *coup de grace*."

It was inescapable; Chantal had somehow found the strength to go back into the cell and bludgeon the unconscious Hansen. I had to admit, my first reaction was one of relief: I had not, after all, killed another human being. Then I thought of Chantal, and the overwhelming rage that must have driven her back into that horror chamber. Did she truly not remember what had happened? If so, what did that close-lipped smile and nod mean a few minutes ago? I felt a chill; my instinctive sympathy for Chantal for all she had undergone was tempered by an amorphous fear. Of her? For Sam? A little of both probably, and also for myself.

"Have you found the video? The surveillance camera in the cell?"

The detective blew air out between pouted lips.

"We have found a large number of video files, a huge amount. It will take days to review them all. We have also taken samples for laboratory analysis from the cell, from

Hansen's living quarters, and his car. Again, it will take a while to obtain complete results. Meanwhile ...." He trailed off, as if wondering whether to confide further information. I silently prayed for Dykstra to keep quiet. I knew his journalistic instincts would lead him to hammer Parmentier with questions, but I sensed that we would learn more by waiting quietly.

"Preliminary findings show ..." He sighed and ran his hands through his unruly grey hair. Just looking at him made me feel exhausted all over again. "Preliminary findings show a link between the woman's body you discovered at Le Bec and the cell where you and Mademoiselle Dubenoit were incarcerated. Also ....," he paused again, "there were other samples found in the cell: hair, finger nails, and so on. I need a sample from you for elimination purposes. Then we can start comparing ..." Another pause.

"With other women who have gone missing," Dykstra completed the thought.

"Yes. I believe you have had a lucky escape, Mademoiselle."

Chapter 20

Sunday

We stopped at the police station for them to take a DNA swab from inside my cheek; then Dykstra and I returned to the hotel. Pierre was waiting in the lobby. For the first time since I met him, he was wearing the dark shirt and clerical collar of a priest. If he saw my surprise, he did not respond to it. His smile embraced us both, and I risked a sideways glance at Dykstra, thinking of his comment earlier that day that Pierre liked me "that way," but his face gave nothing away. He stepped forward to shake Pierre's hand without hesitation this time.

"I came to see how Chantal was doing. And you, too, Sarah, of course." There was a difference that went beyond his clothes. I couldn't put my finger on it. I admitted the possibility that the difference was in me, not him.

"I couldn't speak to her. It seems she's physically OK, but apparently she remembers nothing of what happened at La Bastide." We sat down in the grouping of chairs around the fireplace, and I explained everything that happened at the hospital that morning.

"So they are not going to arrest you for murder?" Pierre asked.

"I don't think so. With the evidence they're gathering against Hansen, it sounds like going against his killer is not a priority. The police are focusing now on identifying his other possible victims. But they haven't finished reviewing all the video from the cell, so …"

Pierre nodded, and we sat in – for me, at least – a somewhat awkward silence, until Pierre pulled a plastic grocery bag up from beside his chair.

"I brought some things for Chantal's father to look at." He held the bag on his knees without opening it. "On Friday, I went into the barn where we found the body. The police finished their examination and took away Chantal's car, so it's no longer a crime scene. I wanted to see what else was stored there. As we thought, it seems to be the contents of the Limoges apartment where Chantal lived with her mother: furniture, books, clothes, and several boxes of papers. As Chantal was still missing on Friday, I thought it was alright to go through the boxes to see if there were any clues to where she might be."

He paused, still holding the bag closed. The priest garb made Pierre look older, and bestowed a quiet authority that kept me from jumping in with questions. Strangely, it appeared to have the same effect on Dykstra, usually not slow to speak.

"I went back this morning to retrieve these. I thought they would help Chantal's father prepare to meet her again after all these years. I haven't read the letters. As you see, they are addressed to him."

As he spoke he withdrew items from the bag and laid them out on the low coffee table in front of us: a photograph album, bound in faded dark blue cloth, and a tin, about eight inches long, five wide and three deep. It was decorated in a floral design, the type of container that might once have held cookies or chocolates. Pierre opened the lid. Inside was a packet of envelopes secured with a rubber band. I saw the word "Papa" on the topmost envelope, written in a neat, compact hand, and reached for the package. I peeled off the band and fanned through the envelopes. Only the top one bore the word "Papa," but when I turned them over I saw that all were sealed closed. They varied in thickness; most appeared to contain several pages. I counted the envelopes.

"Four. I wonder if she gave them to her mother to add the address and mail them, and then Claire hid them away. Or maybe Chantal was writing to some fantasy father. She thinks her father abandoned them – that's what Claire told her. These may be filled with hate." I was thinking out loud, my eyes on the envelopes, still fresh after who knew how many years in their closed container. My instinct was to protect Sam who would be arriving in an hour or so, but I knew he had a right – and a need – to read the enclosures, whatever they contained.

Dykstra slowly leafed through the pages of the album. I put the envelopes back in the tin, and leaned closer to his shoulder. The first pages displayed photos of Chantal as a child, some with her mother, or in a posed classroom group. Her hair was fairer then, worn long in thick untidy curls. There were some other groups and individuals pictured but as none of the photographs had written descriptions, I couldn't guess who they were.

"This was taken at Le Bec," Pierre offered, pointing to a family group around a picnic table, Kodachrome colors now faded to pastel. The grandfather's grin was expansive, his arm possessively around Claire's shoulders. She seemed to be arching away from him, while her mother on his other side smiled weakly at the camera, her eyes caught mid-blink. Chantal, perhaps fifteen years old, was seated at the end of table, next to her grandmother, expression fixed. Her hands were out of sight but, judging from her face, I would lay odds her fists were clenched. I had seen other snapshots like this over the years: family members under orders to look like they're having the time of their lives together, but the moment after the shutter clicks they're either at each other's throats or hurrying off in separate directions. In this photograph, the poses struck by each of the females communicated a tension that was palpable: they didn't want to be there. Only the old man was oblivious, enjoying his role as *pater familias*.

The next pages displayed photographs taken on a trip to Paris – the obligatory shots of a teenage Chantal and her mother posed in front of the Eiffel Tower, the Arc de Triomphe and Notre Dame. The remaining pages in the album were blank, empty of any record of the last twenty-odd years. I wondered if there was another album that Pierre had failed to discover, which continued the story with snaps of later Bastille Day celebrations, birthday parties, and family outings to the countryside. Or were those pages left intentionally blank, as mother and daughter sequestered themselves in the Limoges apartment? At some point, which I calculated to be in the late Eighties, did Claire or Chantal, or both of them, deliberately shun the social rituals typically memorialized with a camera? If so, why? Was their seclusion the result of a specific event, or a slow-growing phobia? Perhaps, when Chantal recovered and was released from hospital she could fill in the missing years for Sam. Perhaps the letters would provide some clues.

Pierre stood up to leave, but hesitated, putting his hands in his pockets, then pulling them out again nervously. He cleared his throat.

"Sarah, er, about this," he gestured quickly at his collar. "I am going to write to my superiors to ask if I can stay and work here, at least for a while. I talked with Father Joseph this morning again after mass. He's getting old and he needs help, especially with the young people in the parish. I think I can be of use." Thinking of the adoring gaze of Jean-Paul's sister, the cashier at the Spar market, I had no doubt he would be more popular with the "young people of the parish" than the irascible curé. "I think also I can be of use to Chantal. When she returns to Le Bec, and after her father goes back to America, she will need someone close by to look after her."

His dark brown eyes shone with a warm intensity that underlined his words. I understood then how easy it had been for Dykstra – and me – to misinterpret him. Pierre cared deeply for others; his natural instinct was to be of service. He had been deeply hurt in Canada when that instinct had boomeranged to make him an outcast. Now, in the *terroir* that had nurtured him as a child, he had found his purpose again.

His urge to help me find Chantal, to track me down after my disappearance, to mediate between me and the police inspector, was selfless; there was no romantic agenda, not even an unconscious one.

"Yes! I'm so glad you—well, you're right. Chantal *will* need a friend, and the parish is lucky to have you!" I peeked at Dykstra. He was looking quizzically at Pierre, head tilted, as if he was having difficulty understanding. I assumed in Dykstra's fast-paced world, the cynical world of the 24-hour news cycle, where "if it bleeds, it leads," this kind of altruism was rare.

***

Sam arrived at about five o'clock, looking even more gaunt and disheveled than when we had last been together in New York. Seeing him peer around the lobby unleashed not only a surge of affection but also a wave of homesickness. Sam was an indelible part of my American life, the predictable existence I had painstakingly crafted for myself in Atlanta, and I wanted it back with an urgency that took me by surprise. In the last week, I barely spared a thought for the hole in my beloved bungalow's roof, for Gerardo as he cleared the debris in preparation for the contractor, or for my upcoming schedule of teaching and mediations. Now, as Dykstra and I led him out to the terrace, I was ready for this adventure to be over and to get back to normality.

But I could not click my heels and magic myself home yet. Dykstra went out for a beer and a prowl around the town, while Sam and I settled ourselves at one of the tables in the shade. It took nearly an hour to catch him up on all that had happened since my last e-mail report. I watched his face reflect surprise, then shock and concern as the story unrolled. I knew jetlag must be mangling his emotions too, so I tried to sound organized and optimistic as I concluded.

"So, we'll meet with Doctor Madjeska at nine tomorrow, before seeing Chantal. I hope we'll get an idea of when Chantal will be released. Then we need to sort out some stuff at Le Bec to get the place ready for her." I was thinking of the mice and the expired foodstuff in the refrigerator. "I expect you'll want to stay with her there, rather than here at the hotel? While we're at the hospital, Dykstra's going to be at the *gendarmerie* and then La Bastide to dig up as much information as he can on the investigation."

Sam drew a deep breath.

"It's ... overwhelming. I don't know what to say, except thank you, of course. Are you okay, Sarah? I never anticipated you would be in danger ..."

"I'm fine, Sam, really. Look, you need sleep, I know, but there's one more thing you should do before tomorrow." I opened the bag Pierre had brought earlier that afternoon and brought out the album and the tin containing the letters.

Sam took his time examining the photographs. I regretted having surrendered the most recent photo of Chantal with Paulette's daughter to the police, but Sam would see her soon enough. When he finally picked up the letters, he turned them over a couple of times, then fanned them out in front of him. I tried to interpret his reluctance to open the envelopes.

"Would you like me to help translate them? Or would you like a nap first, or some food? We can look at them later—"

"No, it's fine, Sarah. I've been working hard at my French since I got back to New York in April. I think I'll take them up to my room and read them there. You and Pieter go out to dinner. I'm not hungry. When you get back, check in with me, and we'll talk. If there's stuff I don't understand, you can help me out then."

I had been insensitive. I had forgotten my earlier speculation that the letters might be hurtful, and reduced them in my mind to a mere puzzle to be deciphered, a missing piece of Chantal's history. Much as I loved him, Sam was not *my* father. He faced an immense challenge; he was going to try to rescue a relationship that had died – if it had ever lived – many years ago. He could only do it alone.

We stood up, and I reached up to kiss his cheek before we headed inside, him to his room, me out through the lobby to find Dykstra.

***

Dykstra was finishing a beer at one of the cafés on the square, looking pretty pleased with himself. He explained, as we strolled to the pizzeria where I had eaten with Pierre earlier in the week. He had stopped by the *gendarmerie* to find that the *procureur* – Parmentier's judicial boss who would supervise the investigation going forward – had finally issued an official statement.

"I'll have the inside track on what looks like might be an international story. The local press will probably pick it up tonight, but I have a running start on the big news outlets!"

I winced inwardly. Of course, this was Dykstra's job, but I dreaded the notoriety, and I was sure that Sam and Chantal could do without it too. We selected a table on the sidewalk, and Dykstra pulled a folded sheet from his pants' pocket.

"They got your name wrong, I'm afraid," *Thank goodness,* I thought, "and they played up the gallant police rescue angle. Here."

I skimmed the print-out. The operative paragraph read: "*Sarah McKenna, an American tourist, and Chantal Dubenoit, long-time Limoges resident who relocated to the area last year, were freed after a daring police raid led by Inspector Dante Alighieri Parmentier, as a result of a tip from a local resident.*" Pierre was not named. "*Torkil Hansen, their presumed captor, died of head injuries sustained during the rescue. No shots were fired.*" That was nicely vague. Inquiring minds might ask how the injuries occurred, but would probably be distracted by the information that followed: "*Forensic evidence gathered at the scene shows that the female whose corpse was found on Tuesday, and is now identified as Isabelle Bernet of La Rochelle, was also held at La Bastide. The autopsy conducted on*

Mademoiselle Bernet shows she died of malnutrition six to eight weeks ago. A complete search of the buildings and grounds is in progress."

"So they haven't found anything yet?"

"No, but I'll be there first thing tomorrow, while you and Sam are at the hospital." He grinned, his eagerness rendering him youthful, but for once his boyish charm did not move me. I was ready to close the book on Hansen and his serial crimes; my focus was already drifting back across the Atlantic. I had one final task to perform: introduce Sam and Chantal, and then …

"You're a million miles away. What's the matter?" Dykstra put his hand over mine, bringing me back to the bustling restaurant. I smiled at him.

"Nothing. I'm fine. What were you saying?"

"I was thinking about what we could do after I've filed the story. Perhaps head south to Bordeaux? Some wine tasting?"

I took a deep breath.

"I don't think so. It feels like I've been away so long. I just want to go home."

His eyes filled with sadness, and for a moment I regretted my words, but I did not withdraw them. He leaned forward and kissed me gently, then lifted my hand and kissed that too, and kept it prisoner against his cheek.

"Poor Sarah, you have been through so much."

I could feel tears pricking my eyelids. I blinked away the self-pity, grateful to see the waiter approaching with our order.

***

I tapped on Sam's door; Dykstra stood at my shoulder carrying the leftover slices of pizza wrapped in foil. Sam's face, when he opened for us, looked dazed. I wondered whether it was jetlag, the contents of Chantal's letters, or a combination of both. He gestured for us to sit. Dykstra took the only chair, and I perched on the edge of the bed, careful not to disturb the papers.

He had arranged the contents of the envelopes in piles across the bed. I saw that only the first could properly be called a letter; it began "*Cher Papa,*" a single page, formally arranged with the Limoges address and the date at the top. The others – each consisting of several pages, close-covered with writing – had no addressee.

Sam paced, absent-mindedly unwrapping the pizza and taking a bite, He chewed, swallowed and then spoke, reminding me of Marta in her professorial mode.

"This first letter was written in 1982, a little less than a year after Marta and I visited Chantal in Limoges." He picked it up and handed it to me to read, but continued to explain its contents. "She says she is disappointed not to have heard from me, especially on her birthday which was the week before." His voice suddenly took on a quaver. "But I had written to her, and sent gifts at Christmas, as well as her birthday!" He regained control. "As you see, the rest is stuff about her school, the weather … At the end, she says she hopes to come and stay with me in New York. I had been asking and asking Claire to arrange a trip! Chantal was thirteen, old enough to travel alone, but Claire never responded. I never heard from either of them!" He was getting emotional. I put the letter back on the bed and picked up the next pile of paper.

"So, this is three years later. Not addressed to me, although I am referenced in it. She's angry, mostly at her mother, but some at me. '*She never lets me do anything I want! I hate her! If only I could go live with Papa!*' I guess that's typical teenage rebellion. What do you think?"

I shrugged. With my history, I couldn't comment on typical teenage behavior, but there didn't seem anything particularly unusual about the two pages of rant. Apparently, she was not happy at school either. Maybe she was a victim of bullying. One thing I did remember was how cruel teenage girls can be to anyone a little different.

"Then there's this." Sam exchanged the pages I was holding with the next sheaf. "Look at the newspaper cutting first."

Paper-clipped to the back of the pages was a newspaper obituary column dated February 20, 1990.

"*Henri Dubenoit, aged seventy, after a short illness ....*"

Grandpère Dubenoit was, according to the memorial article, a dentist, a devoted husband and father, pillar of the church and leading member of several civic associations in Limoges, beloved of patients, friends and family alike.

"*I thought she would be glad he was dead; she despised him so much. But when I said as much to her, she looked at me strangely. Now she has shut herself up in her bedroom, and it is left to me to shop, to cook, to clean. Yes, now I'm the maid too. She insisted I tell Madame Debus not to come anymore. She can't stand the noise of buckets and mops and vacuum cleaner! She is so selfish!*"

Reading between the lines of Chantal's complaints that meandered on for a couple of pages, Claire was suffering from depression.

"*I am a prisoner of her illness – is it real or imagined? – I don't know and it doesn't matter: she rules my life like a tyrant, all the time pretending she loves me, that it is for my protection, I'm too fragile to go out into the world, to work, to meet people, have friends. It isn't me that's fragile, it's her – she's too afraid to try life. She did once and all she got from that was me. I'm the punishment for her single attempt at independence.*"

So this was the start of the blank album pages: Chantal's missing years. She was twenty-one years old, her mother's prisoner. Another paragraph caught my eye:

"*She's so beautiful. Even now, even though I detest her, it's a pleasure to look at her. Black hair, white skin, cheek bones like angels' wings, a neck like a swan's. But I came out malformed, misshapen. Was that my father's contribution? I don't remember him as ugly, but then I hardly remember him at all. Maman says he's very smart; that is all she will say in his favor, and from her even that doesn't sound like a compliment. 'He abandoned us.' 'He married someone else.' 'He isn't interested in you.' Who could blame him? I'm not smart like him, and I'm not beautiful like her."*

I handed the pages to Dykstra, and we sat in silence while he read. There was one set of pages left on the bed. Sam rested his hand on it as if reluctant to share its contents.

"There's no date on this. I think it was written at different times – see, she used different pens – but it was probably during the last couple of years when Claire was ill, and she wrote the last bit after Claire died." He handed me the pages. "I think I understand but I'd like your interpretation."

Chantal's tone was quite different in these later writings. The anger and frustration she expressed at the narrow confines of her life had calmed into a reflective mood. Had she come to terms, and learned to accept her mother's "protection"? It was improbable that she could spend twenty years raging.

"I love children. I like to go to the park and watch them play on the swings. Maman frowns at me, and says I'll be arrested as a pervert. She doesn't like me to leave the apartment, jealous of anything that draws my attention away from her. It would be no use explaining; she can't understand anyone's feelings but her own. I don't go to watch the happy children, the ones that scream and giggle and hold each others' hands. There's always one at the side, one that hangs back with eyes on the ground, afraid to join in because she might be rejected. That's the one I watch. That's me, the outsider, the lonely one ...."

I looked up at Sam who had taken a seat on the bed next to me and was reading silently along with me. He smiled sadly, and encouraged me to continue with a nod of the head.

"No man will want me now. Forty years old. I look at my soft white stomach, my thighs blotched and flabby, toe nails already thickening like an old person's. What happened? How did I lose twenty years of life? I hate the mirror. It shows my bulldog jaw, my reddened cheeks and,

yes, the strands of grey in my unruly hair. No one would want me now, except a freak.

I dream of a lover who comes in the night. Darkness would cloak my ugliness. He would take me – quickly – and leave me pregnant. Pregnant with a baby that had his beauty, none of my imperfections. And so, against every instinct, I wish to copy my mother: a stranger comes and leaves a gift. But while Maman saw the gift as penance, I would embrace it as my just reward.

There will be no dream lover ...."

The last page was in a different ink.

"Maman refused to see a doctor. She complained of headaches, and would not let me open the shutters; only candlelight was soft enough for her eyes. She refused to even lift her head to sip the tisane I made. I thought she was willing herself to die, but then she became anxious, fastening her hand around my wrist with a ferocious grip. She wanted to make her confession. When I tried to free myself to telephone the priest, she said, no, she was going to confess to me.

I don't want her secrets. She told me horrible, unspeakable things. I don't know if they are true or hallucinations created by her diseased brain. If Grandpère was really the monster she described why did she come back to Limoges? Why did she let him support her? Why did we go to his house for Christmas and Réveillon, and to Le Bec in the summer?

Now she is dead, I will draw a curtain across, as if everything before has been wiped clean. I am starting fresh, free to do what I want. It is not *too late."*

I held my eyes fixed on the sheets on my lap for a while after I finished reading, trying to sort through my reactions, to see the whole saga laid out by Chantal's writings objectively, not injecting conclusions drawn from my own history. I was moved by the courage of her last declaration; she had set out at mid-life to build a new existence. Instead, she had stumbled into the path of a psychopath. But beating insistently behind my sympathy for Chantal was the inference that Claire had been a victim of abuse. Did that explain her withdrawal from society, her obsessive need to keep her daughter close, even her inability to make a marriage work with someone I knew to be one of the most lovable men on the planet?

"Did you suspect any of this?" I asked Sam, pointing at the final paragraphs.

"No, nothing. When I first met Claire, she was a free spirit. She changed in New York after Chantal was born. I assumed it was post-partum depression, plus homesickness. I was young and inexperienced. I guess I really didn't know her well at all."

"Poor Claire. Poor Chantal. They've been through so much." I realized I had echoed Dykstra's words about me earlier in the evening. I wasn't sure who my tears were for this time.

Chapter 21

Monday

Sam and I were strung tight with nerves as we entered the hospital the next morning. For me, this was the culmination of a quest. I should have been pleased with myself. In the last week, I had faced a disorienting array of experiences, all literally foreign to my everyday existence. I had survived them, and was about to achieve my object of introducing Sam to his estranged daughter. Instead of feeling satisfaction and relief, I could not stop my mind from picking away at the remaining ambiguities: how profoundly had Chantal been damaged? Would Sam be hurt by this longed-for reunion? Did the ongoing criminal investigation mean I wasn't free to go home?

Beyond these immediate concerns were nagging questions about my relationship with Dykstra. I seemed programmed to push him away the moment he wanted more closeness. After years of carefully distancing myself from lovers who might want more from me than sex, I had fallen for Dykstra the previous September. Back then, I congratulated myself that head had triumphed over hormones when I scotched the idea of a long-term relationship. Going to bed with him again in New York was either a huge mistake or a mad grab at my last chance at happiness. Was my urge to fly back to Georgia a rational need to regroup, or a desperate attempt to escape emotional commitment?

Sam had said little before we parted the night before, but I suspected that Chantal's writings had shaken him. He had probably re-read them before sleeping, trying to glean all he could about her temperament. Now, he looked even more hollow-eyed and tense. He remained silent as we found our way up to the third floor and Sylvia Madjeska's office.

Doctor Madjeska's English was correct, although her words had the hard curl of a Polish accent, and I needed to concentrate to understand her. I thought her arrogant the day before, but that may have been the impression she gave of looking down her nose – a prominent Roman one – from her above-average height. Today, seated behind her desk, her approach was merely cautious.

"Monsieur Cantor, do you have evidence of your relationship with Chantal Dubenoit?"

Luckily, Sam had anticipated this, and produced, as well as his passport, copies of his marriage certificate to Claire Dubenoit issued by the Borough of Manhattan, and Chantal's birth certificate dated March 22, 1969. It named him and Claire as parents.

She examined the documents carefully before handing them back.

"Your daughter was badly dehydrated when she arrived. She is also malnourished and has poor muscle tone. We found no other serious physical injuries or evidence of recent physical trauma, but we conducted a battery of tests to make sure there was no underlying infection or disease present." The doctor paused to open the file in front of her. I was expecting her to talk about the test results, but instead she closed the file again, and leaned back in her chair. "What she needs now is good, regular meals, plenty of rest, and moderate exercise – walking, for example."

I sensed she was avoiding something, or maybe weighing up how to express it. I looked over at Sam. His voice was outwardly calm, but his knee jumped rapidly up and down below the level of the desk.

"You've described her physical condition, but how is she, emotionally? Sarah said a psychological assessment was done."

Doctor Madjeska seemed relieved that Sam had broached the topic.

"Yes. That's standard in cases like this, kidnap victims, victims of abuse... However, it's not like a blood test; there is no quantifiable result, no obvious diagnosis. We know so little, you see. Chantal claims to have no memory of what happened during her imprisonment—"

" 'Claims'? Does that mean you think she *does* remember?"

"No, no. I should have said she *reports* having no memory. Sometimes, victims suffer from traumatic amnesia. This seems to be such a case. The memories of what happened may return over time; we can't predict that. What the assessment shows is that so far, Chantal is coping well: no hysteria, no obvious symptoms of depression. However, continued regular psychological counseling is recommended. And she will need a stable, supportive environment, with minimal stress. How long are you able to stay here, Monsieur Cantor?"

"As long as she needs me."

"But what about the Center?" I spoke for the first time since entering the doctor's office, but broke off at a glance from Sam. His look contained more than a hint of reproach, and I felt humbled. He had been almost completely absent from Chantal's life so far; of course, he would want to remedy that.

Sam stood up, eager now to meet his daughter. I rose too, but the doctor remained seated.

"There is something else."

We sat again, and watched as she reopened the file in front of her.

"As I said, we did tests: blood, urine, a full physical examination ….. Monsieur Cantor, your daughter is pregnant." The word hung in the air between us; the doctor's exaggeratedly rolled 'r' and the extra syllable after the 'g' transforming it momentarily into the name of some bizarre disorder. Comprehension dawned as she continued. "A month, six weeks at most. It is therefore probable that she conceived while she was held captive." She raised her eyes to Sam's, and waited for him to fully absorb the information. I felt detached, as if I was watching a play; this seemed so unreal, a plot twist in a television drama, a manufactured cliff-hanger to keep the viewer enthralled until next week's episode. Then, just as suddenly, I thought of the dead woman in Chantal's car. She had a name now: Isabelle Bernet. She had been pregnant too. I remembered the smell, the skittering mouse, and I wanted to be sick.

"Does she know?" Sam's voice came out in a croaking whisper.

"Yes. That is, I have told her. She seems ... accepting. But she is still recovering from her ordeal. We have not discussed courses of action. There is time to decide, but that is a conversation you should have with her soon."

An abortion. Her inference was clear. But the doctor had not read the confessions Chantal had hidden in the cookie tin. She did not know about the long years of self-denial spent looking after her mother, and she had not seen the photograph Chantal commissioned of herself and Paulette's little girl. What was it Chantal wrote about her "dream lover"? *A stranger comes and leaves a gift. But while Maman saw the gift as penance, I would embrace it as my just reward.*

This time, it was Doctor Madjeska who rose first, while we sat motionless, still dazed by her news.

"It'll be alright," I murmured to Sam, taking his hand and encouraging him to his feet. I had no grounds for thinking so, other than my faith in Sam's innate goodness and wisdom. We followed the doctor out to the nurses' station where she shook our hands and indicated the direction of Chantal's room.

"Do you want me to wait outside?" I asked.

"No!" Sam looked panicked. "Please stay with me."

Chantal looked composed, propped up against the pillows, and again wearing a green hospital gown that did nothing for her complexion. She greeted us with a nod.

I spoke first.

"*Bonjour*, Chantal. How are you? It's Sarah; do you remember me? And this is Sam, your father, arrived from America. I told you he was coming, remember?" I spoke slowly for Sam's benefit, while carefully monitoring her reaction. I found it hard to believe she was suffering from amnesia. How could she forget what was still so sharply etched into *my* consciousness? I wanted to prod her into admitting she knew me, but she just nodded again, and switched her unwavering gaze to Sam.

"Chantal, it's been so long since we met. I'm so sorry … for everything. I am here now and I will stay here."

"My papa? How is it possible? You are an old man!" Then she smiled, a real one this time, not the closed-lip smirk she had graced me with yesterday. Sam and I both laughed in relief as the tension lifted.

"Yes! You're right, I'm an old man!" Sam began to reminisce in his fractured French about the last time he had seen her, asking no questions that required much of a response from her, smoothly switching gears to chat about Le Bec, life in the country compared to Limoges, what she wanted to do once she was home from hospital. I sat quietly, smiling in admiration; he seemed quite at ease, and so, strangely, did Chantal. Sam had spent a career diffusing stressful situations, but I would not have imagined his daughter to possess the social skills to respond to his efforts.

She lifted a hand to interrupt him.

"Sam – may I call you that? 'Papa' seems rather childish – would you mind if I talked to Sarah? Privately, I mean?"

Sam was non-plussed, as was I, but he recovered quickly.

"Of course not. I'll go find some coffee."

The door closed behind him, and I turned to Chantal inquiringly, just in time to see the affability drain from her face.

"I want you to leave."

"What? But you said you wanted to talk to me—"

"I mean, leave France. Leave us alone. Go back to America."

Her edict kicked me in the stomach like a mule. Although I had decided the day before that I would head out as soon as the police approved my departure, and had even gone online to research possible flights, my eagerness for home was conditioned on Sam not needing me anymore. To be summarily kicked out, after all my efforts, was not part of the game plan. However, after a moment's reflection, I shouldered past my hurt vanity. Chantal seemed to be morphing from victim to predator in front of my eyes. What was Sam taking on here?

"Why don't you want me here, Chantal? Is it because I know what happened to you at La Bastide? But I won't talk to anyone about that. Not Sam, or anyone, I promise."

"You think you know," she hissed. "But you don't! The things the inspector says I told you, it's just hearsay. I can't confirm or deny it, and he's dead so there will be no trial."

"Hansen's dead, yes. But what about the physical evidence and the surveillance camera?"

One look at her face told me she had forgotten about the video. Chantal had not had my years of practice in cloaking her thoughts. Her realization about what the camera might have recorded demonstrated that her amnesia was faked. But that didn't explain why she faked it. I gave her a moment to reassemble her defenses.

"The psychiatrist says there was nothing I could have done to save myself; none of it was my fault." She sounded petulant now.

"Of course not; it wasn't your fault." I of all people should have seen it: the victim who blames herself, and, rather than deal with the guilt, deliberately distances herself from anything that might remind her of the ordeal. Of course, she *had* bludgeoned Hansen to death, but I was cautious about confronting her with that fact.

"So, you'll leave?"

"Yes, as soon as I can."

"Thank you. You can get Sam." I was at the door when she spoke again in a low voice, as if to herself. "He'll understand. We have to think what is best for the baby now."

After Sam came back into the hospital room, Chantal chatted animatedly about the future, referring more than once to "*le bébé*." She had drawn a curtain across the past, and was starting fresh, as she had pledged to do after her mother's death. I had done the same once, so who was I to judge her? But her fresh start involved me abandoning my best friend. How could I best help him?

***

Sam did not ask about my private conversation with Chantal, and I didn't volunteer anything. I wanted to think through Chantal's request – more of a demand, really – before broaching the subject, or discussing the challenges he might face in taking on her care. We drove in near silence from Montbrun back to Le Bec where we planned to do some cleaning and make an inventory of what was needed for Chantal's return there, perhaps as soon as the following day.

Happily, Pierre was at home when we pulled up in front of the farmhouse. He came out, drying his hands on a dish towel, dressed again in shorts and tee shirt. I felt more comfortable with *this* Pierre than yesterday's formally-garbed priest. I dismissed the thought that my ease might also have something to do with Dykstra's absence.

"I was making lunch. Come in!"

As I anticipated, Sam and Pierre warmed to each other immediately. I carried plates and a basket of bread out to the terrace, while Pierre tossed a salad and directed Sam to unwrap a selection of cheeses.

After we served ourselves and Pierre poured us each a glass of a crisp *rosé de Provence,* he turned to Sam.

"How is Chantal?"

I was eager to hear Sam's response, and glad I had postponed my own questions until some space and time had intervened between us and this morning's disturbing meeting.

"She is …. remarkable. I keep thinking of Sleeping Beauty or Rapunzel: those folk tales where the princess is imprisoned for years, and then emerges to live happily ever after. But Chantal emerged from one prison to enter another. She seems untouched in a way, as if she can summon her "happily ever after" by pure effort of will. Of course, you haven't read her writings, Pierre: the contents of the box you found in the barn. She wanted a child, and, hey presto, she's going to have one."

Pierre's face registered shock.

"She's pregnant?"

"Yes. I don't think we will ever know what exactly happened during those first weeks at La Bastide. Hansen raped her … or seduced her. Anyway, she's determined to look only forwards."

"She's keeping the child?"

Sam nodded, and Pierre looked relieved. I remembered Rebekah's story; what a weird world of parallels we live in.

After lunch, Pierre gave us the key and we went next door. Intrepid woman I may be, but I let Sam handle the rodent problem before retrieving some cleaning utensils from under the stairs. Then I rewashed the sheets and towels that had been languishing in the machine since April, and hung them out to dry in the sanitizing sunshine.

As we dusted and mopped our way through the house, Sam opened up about his emotions.

"I can't help feeling guilty. I should have intervened long ago, when Claire stopped communicating with me. If Chantal had a more normal life she wouldn't have been so vulnerable. I wish I had known that Claire was so …"

"Crazy?"

"Ha! We're not supposed to use that word, but yes. I suppose now it hardly matters whether her mental issues were a result of childhood abuse, except that it does suggest a cycle: generation to generation." Sam paused his mopping, a frown shadowing his face.

"But you are here now to break the cycle," I reminded him gently. "I agree with Chantal in this, at least: the past is past. We can't change it. But you will ensure this baby has the best start possible. Chantal will get counseling, and Pierre is here to help—"

My cell phone interrupted us. I pulled it out of my back pocket.

"Dykstra."

"Hi, Sarah. I'm at the *mairie*, waiting for a press conference to start. Where are you?"

I briefly recounted our day, and promised to meet him at the police station when we finished at Le Bec. I knew another interview with Inspector Parmentier would be necessary before I could firm up my flight out the next day. If I was cleared to leave, I would miss the *Fête de Musique,* but *tant pis*, there would be other years. I nurtured a gleam of hope that, under Sam's benign influence, Chantal would lift her lifetime ban on my presence in France.

***

The press conference was over when Sam dropped me off, before heading back to the hotel for a nap. Dykstra had walked back from the relative opulence of the *mairie,* and was waiting for me in the unfriendly reception area of the *gendarmerie*. His face lit up when he saw me. I thought drily that it was probably not my appearance that excited him, as much as the new information gleaned from the police.

"The dogs found human remains buried at La Bastide; two women, dead some time, maybe years. No DNA identification yet, and the autopsy results will take another day at least, but one of them was pregnant!"

The acrid taste of bile rose into the back of my throat. I swallowed, smiled, and changed the subject.

"I'm going to check in with the inspector to find out if I'm cleared to leave town. Was there any news about the video records?"

"Yes. They finished reviewing them, and can confirm that the body in the barn, Isabel Bernet, died in that cell. They didn't say anything about video of you and Chantal, though."

"Hmm. I'll find out from Parmentier."

Dykstra wanted to come with me to the inspector's office, but a policewoman firmly dissuaded him. He fell into the press camp now, and had no rights to inside information.

Inspector Parmentier looked even more rumpled than before. A full ashtray and a string of empty coffee cups testified to the long hours he had spent on the investigation.

"Asseyez-vous, s'il vous plait."

I took the chair across the desk from him, and carefully laid out my plans to return to the U.S. the following day.

"Is there anything else you need from me before I leave?"

We both knew I was skirting the issue: would I be prosecuted for my part in Hansen's death?

"He stopped the video."

"What?" I didn't understand what he was saying.

"Before he entered the cell to determine if you were dead, he stopped recording. It was a pattern. All the video shows – hours of it – are his prisoners. The camera never shows him. So there is insufficient evidence to determine how he died. It may have been an accident."

I looked at him, speechless. He gazed back, smiling slightly. I should leave well alone, but the lawyer in me persisted.

"What if Chantal eventually regains her memory?"

He shrugged – that Gallic shrug again – and levered himself to his feet.

"The death of Torkil Hansen is a closed case. His crimes, however, are still under investigation. Your statement was very helpful, and complete. I wish you *bon voyage!*"

We shook hands, and I went to find Dykstra.

Chapter 22

Tuesday

It was not my choice to spend another minute in the bland waiting room at the hospital, but Sam was reluctant to stray far from Chantal's bedside. The off-white walls, sputtering fluorescent light, and absence of any artwork except a crucifix and a grim *"Défense de Fumer!"* sign conspired to depress the spirit. I sensed a miasma of misery hanging in the air from all the bad news shared in this place: *I'm sorry to inform you ... The prognosis is not good .... The surgery did not go as planned ...* The visitors' room at a federal penitentiary would be more cheerful.

Dykstra was driving my rental car. He had dropped me off, and then headed out to La Bastide where the search for more graves continued. He hoped to nab another interview with Inspector Parmentier before he filed his story. He would pick me up at noon with plenty of time to make my two-thirty p.m. flight out of Limoges Airport. I paced the beige vinyl floor, glad of these moments alone to consider the right note to strike in my goodbyes to Sam.

His decision to stay in France and care for Chantal and her baby did not surprise me, but I worried for him. She was damaged in so many and profound ways that I suspected she might never be able to form a healthy relationship with her father or anyone else. I feared she would drain him dry, emotionally and financially. Far from his New York City home and his life's work at the Dispute Resolution Center, he would have no support system to sustain him other than Pierre. But this was hardly the moment to predict doom and gloom. My role was to bolster his confidence and congratulate him on his new-found family.

I came to rest in front of a toy basket in the corner. Forlorn stuffed animals lolled tiredly in its depths, the pile topped by a battered baby doll, painted blue eyes staring fixedly up at the water-stained ceiling panels. Sam came up behind me and wrapped an arm around my shoulders.

"It's not too late for you, Sarah. I mean, you and Dykstra—"

I followed the direction of his gaze towards the toy basket.

"What? No! I don't want a child! That's ridiculous!" I saw in his eyes that I had hurt him. "I'm sorry, it's just that I don't think I'd be a good mother. I lack …. the skills." I finished lamely. This was a line I had fallen back on in the past when others extolled the joys of parenthood.

Sam led me to the row of hard plastic chairs against the wall, and we sat in silence for some moments before he spoke.

"Marta and I wanted children, but she couldn't conceive. We looked at adoption, but, when it came to it, I couldn't commit. I backed out. I regret it now, but then I felt I had already failed as a father – with Chantal. I couldn't take the risk of failing again. Now, I have another chance, not just with Chantal—"

He broke off and turned to face me, leveling his brows in a look of stern determination that would have been comical in another situation.

"She's determined to keep the child. It may not be the wisest choice: a baby from rape, that psychopath's genes. But it's her decision, and I am here to support her."

"Sam! You'll be … you *are* a wonderful father. I wish you were *my* father."

Deep inside, I felt a dam break, and tears jumped from my eyes. I swiped them away furiously but they still coursed down my cheeks.

"Tell me about it."

"I can't!" I gulped. I had never told Sam the details of my early life, or Dykstra either, for that matter. They knew it had been unhappy, and I had taken advantage of an American family connection to escape, and gain an education and a new identity in the States. Telling more awakened memories I didn't wish to revisit, and invited questions to which I had no answers. Were my parents still alive? Did they ever try to find me? What happened to my half-brother?

"Yes, you can, Sarah." His voice was serene, low and calming. "I think it might be a relief to talk. And I'm safe." He smiled. "You know me; I don't judge."

I stood on the edge of a dark pool. Sam might be the devil inviting me to a death by drowning – drowning in bottomless self-pity and loss of control. Once I opened Pandora's box, I feared I'd be overwhelmed with emotions that would blow me apart. Or he might point the way to liberation. I just might be able to swim away from secrecy and self-loathing to a place where I could form relationships unfettered by shame.

Sam handed me a box of tissues and I blew my nose noisily.

"It's hard …"

"Mmm."

A hospital orderly stuck his head around the door, saw the two of us slumped together in our seats, and retreated quickly. His footsteps reverberated down the corridor, and I stepped back from the edge. No, this was not the time or place, but if I ever confided in anyone, it would be this man. I gripped his hand.

"Sam, I can't, but you mustn't worry about me. I'll tell you this much: I was lucky. When I was thirteen, I ran away. Social Services placed me with a foster mother, Margaret Mumford. She fought for me: a scholarship, my US passport. I changed my name, my accent, everything." I managed a bitter chuckle. "I became Sarah McKinney, a new person."

"Sarah, I wish…" Sam didn't complete his thought. He didn't need to. I was thinking the same: I wish I'd been *his* daughter. We sat for a few minutes longer, holding hands and giving an occasional squeeze to let each other know we cared. If anyone could put together Chantal's broken parts, and help her raise a healthy child, it was Sam.

***

Dykstra must have seen that I'd been crying when he picked me up at the hospital's main entrance, but I was grateful that he said nothing, and we rode in silence for several minutes. I thought over the parallels and differences between Chantal and me. We had both suffered, and while the childhood sexual and physical abuse I had undergone was objectively worse than the psychological scars her mother inflicted on her, I had escaped earlier. She had lost, not just her childhood, but her entire young adulthood in virtual imprisonment, and when she finally emerged, she was so vulnerable that she fell prey to a psychopathic killer. I must have sighed deeply; Dykstra reached a hand over to grasp mine, but he kept his silence.

He wanted to keep the rental car another couple of days until he wrapped up the story, but the officious woman at the Hertz desk insisted I turn in the car and he rent another in his own name. After we switched his bags over to the trunk of the new rental, he walked me over to the terminal, and I checked in. We had time to purchase coffee and sandwiches for a late lunch before I would need to go through to the gate.

"Would you like to see what I turned in?" He opened his laptop and cleared a space in front of me on the café table. "It should hit the wire this afternoon, and be in tomorrow's print editions. The TV news folks will already be on their way in."

Mass murder was not Dykstra's type of story. He wrote about international politics, specializing in the Middle East, but he was the man on the spot and a good journalist. His psychological profile of Torkil Hansen was impressively complete, given the short time available. As agreed, he had downplayed my role in the rescue: "*A concerned friend whose determined search put her own life in danger."* He was discreet too about Chantal who was *"recovering in hospital after being reunited with her family."* Sam could be relied on to protect Chantal going forward; I imagined him dealing politely but firmly with any media intrusion. Although the remains found in the two graves at La Bastide had not yet been identified – other than that they were female and had been dead for more than six months – the story confirmed that the body found a week ago in a barn near Saint Barthélemy was Isabelle Bernet, thirty-nine years old, who had disappeared from La Rochelle in October of the previous year. *"Forensic and other evidence link her to La Bastide."* A sinister twilight shot of La Bastide and an old file photograph of Hansen looking like a teenage Andy Warhol accompanied the article.

"Hansen's big mistake was taking the corpse to Le Bec," I said "He should have buried her at La Bastide like the others."

"He thought he was taking care of several problems at once: getting rid of the body and Chantal's car, and clearing out her house. I think he kept his excursions outside La Bastide to a minimum, and probably changed his appearance each time. No, his big mistake was underestimating you, Sarah."

"I don't think so. If anyone deserves credit, it's probably Chantal. She was supposed to keep everything about her new job secret, but she mentioned La Bastide to the curé. What about Parmentier? Maybe he'd enjoy the media attention?"

Dykstra laughed.

"Well, I think he understands he's in an embarrassing position because he brushed off Chantal's disappearance. I suspect he'll be careful not to claim too much limelight."

As he put away the computer, I looked at my watch; I should be moving. Before I could speak, Dykstra leaned forward and trapped my hands between his.

"Sarah – no, don't say anything. This was all supposed to be different. I planned for us to spend time together here. We've never really had a chance just to be lovers, to enjoy each other's company—"

"Good food, good wine ..." I teased him gently.

"Yes, that too." He grinned, but then turned serious. "The thing is ... I want you to know ... when you were missing, I was so scared... I don't want to lose you. I love you."

I think I stopped breathing, and I could feel tears leaking down my cheeks again. I opened my mouth but, for once, no words came. I had always avoided the L word, perhaps because I didn't know what it meant – to the person using it, or to me. Suddenly, looking into Dykstra's eyes, it made sense. *This* was love: this leap of faith across all the barriers we stupid humans erect to keep us from getting hurt – that *I* had erected, time and again, pushing Dykstra away emotionally, even when I wanted him physically.

I kissed him hard, teeth, tongue, hands grabbing. We stood up, coffee cups flying, needing to glue our bodies together, to never let go. Customers gasped, ironic clapping from one.

"I love you too," I whispered into his ear when my breath gave out and our lips reluctantly parted. "We can make this work—"

"Shhh. Just kiss me again." I complied. He was right. Atlanta versus London, his career versus my career: it didn't matter. The moment mattered. Opening my heart to love mattered.

"Air France annonce le départ immédiat du vol quarante dix-sept à Paris-Charles de Gaulle."

"I have to go." We walked hand-in-hand towards the security checkpoint. "When will I see you again?"

"Very soon, I promise. Call me as soon as you land."

Another long kiss, and then he was hidden behind the automatic doors. I went through security in a daze, and found my gate.

***

Half an hour later, the plane banked to make its turn north to Paris. The countryside spread out beneath us: gold and green fields neatly bordered by dark hedgerows, farms and villages like children's toys fresh from the box, pristine and tidy. A river wound across the landscape, reflecting sunlight, a silvery snake insinuating its way through Eden. We leveled out and entered a cloud bank, and the Dordogne vanished like a dream.

Dykstra said we would see each other again soon, but when? In a few weeks I would start teaching my law school class. His U.S. book tour was over; he would have no work-related reason to cross the Atlantic for a while. Perhaps Christmas? Six months with nothing but phone calls and e-mails! That reminded me of his request to call him as soon as I landed. Did he mean in Paris – less than an hour's flight away -- or when I finally arrived home in Atlanta? But that would be in the middle of the night in France. The lightness of being that had buoyed me since my conversation with Sam dissipated into my usual practice of over-thinking things.

"*Salope!*" The insult penetrated easily from the seat behind mine, but I could not make out the stream of intensely whispered French that followed. No response from his seatmate.

I had noticed them during boarding. He was muscular, dark oily hair, wet lips and hairy arms. Not my type, although I knew some women went for it. She looked older, maybe forty; bleached blond hair, super-skinny, Jackie-O sunglasses. Silence now, but I felt the tension hum between them. I wondered about their relationship. How long had they been together? What provoked his outburst and why didn't she defend herself? Pointless musings, but they served to distract me from examining my own romantic situation.

Not really. An anonymous passenger, thirty thousand feet above the planet, I faced the truism that everywhere you go, there you are. Second-guessing myself was second nature to me. Would Dykstra and I turn into the couple in the row behind in two or three years, each staring away into a separate distance, mentally rehearsing recriminations? *You always .... Why can't you .... I should never have ....*

I must have sighed more audibly than I intended. The elderly woman next to me turned and smiled, bright blue eyes twinkling.

"I love flying, don't you?" She said in British-accented English. "It's so liberating."

I couldn't help but smile back. The PA system announced our initial approach to Paris-Charles de Gaulle. My companion tilted her head to listen to the English translation.

"'Better to travel hopefully than to arrive,' they say!"

"As long as we *do* arrive," I replied.

She laughed. "But how do you *know* when you've arrived? I'm eighty-three, and I haven't arrived yet!"

I pondered her comments as I dutifully raised my seat to an upright and locked position, and checked the security of my seat-belt. *Traveling hopefully*: that described Chantal and Sam, as they embarked together on the difficult task of forging a family out of the ruins of past relationships and recent trauma.

It could describe Dykstra and me, too, if I let it.

Praise for *A Slippery Slope*, the first Sarah McKinney mystery:

"A well-paced, engrossing mystery ... The prose is especially elegant ... A suspenseful, intelligent debut mystery novel"

Kirkus Reviews

FOR MORE ABOUT THE AUTHOR AND THE SARAH MCKINNEY SERIES:

Go to www.marianexall.com

Made in the USA
Lexington, KY
09 June 2015